The Trail of the Seneca

James A. Braden

The Trail Of The Seneca

CHAPTER I – THE BEGINNING OF IT ALL

A hatchet of stone, cumbersome and crude, but a dangerous weapon once, though now it is only a silent memento of the days of Captain Pipe, of Lone-Elk, of Fishing Bird, the scowling Big Buffalo and the graceful, pretty Gentle Maiden as well, lies on my table as I write.

Of Captain Pipe, Big Buffalo and certain of the others, I have already told you something; – but you have yet to hear of Lone-Elk, the Seneca, – Lone-Elk, the outcast from the villages of his people, – bold and strong yet crafty, deceitful, treacherous, – and still, withal as ambitious and as vain an Indian as ever trod the long-ago forest fastnesses.

It is of Lone-Elk that I am to tell you now. What part this tomahawk, which lies upon my table, had in the story may later be revealed to you, but as for that, it is not of great soon to feel the awful force of his evil power, calmly fished from their canoe at the opposite side of the water.

Never before had the Delawares prepared so lavishly for the fall Thanksgiving. To celebrate the Festival of the Harvest when the corn and the beans and the squashes, the tobacco and the nuts had been gathered in was no new thing among them, but Lone-Elk had made the plans for a far more elaborate entertainment this year than the people of Captain Pipe's village were accustomed to have. And notwithstanding that the Seneca was a wanderer from his own home country and might never go back to his rightful tribe, the chief of the Delawares had allowed him to assume the leadership in every arrangement for the happy occasion.

However, Lone-Elk well knew how best to prepare all things to please and favor Captain Pipe, and he did not fail to see to it that the latter was given many opportunities to display his dignity and his eloquence and wisdom in the speech-making and addresses to the spirits during the exercises in the Council House. What could be more natural, then, than that the head Delaware should refuse to listen to those of his people who would have criticised the policy of allowing a comparative stranger' to direct and lead them?

The wandering October breezes scarcely rippled the waters of the little lake. They whispered in the half-bare branches of the trees and seemed to play at hide-and-seek with the fallen leaves. The blue smoke curling up from the hole in the roof of the Council House was scarcely moved by them. All was serenely quiet in and about the Indian town on this autumn day in the year 1792, excepting only in the Council House itself, where all the Delawares and even a few Mingoes, or stragglers from other tribes or towns, were come together for Thanksgiving. All had come but one.

Even the most ardent of the young braves had put aside their talk of war — all summer long they had talked of little else — to participate in the celebration, and each had brought a contribution of meat of his own killing for the feast which was to follow the speech-making and offerings to the Great Spirit. All the youngsters, the boys and girls of the village, were there. The old men and women, also, were present. Captain Pipe of course was there and Fishing Bird and Long Hair and Little Wolf. Of all the people of the town upon the lake only one was missing from the ceremonies.

A solemn scene it was when Hopocon, or Pipe, for the former was his Indian name, in his imposing chieftain's costume stood before the little fire in the center of the long, low bark building and sprinkled broken tobacco leaves upon the coals that their incense rising might bear his words on high. It was an impressive scene as well, and though the number present was large, the greatest quiet prevailed.

It was also an interesting sight. The warriors and bucks were in their brightest and newest kilts, leggins and moccasins, with braided belts bound like sashes about their waists or over their shoulders. Some wore the head-dress of colored eagle feathers; some did not. Lone-Elk was of the former and in addition a piece of silver, supported by a cord of leather

3

about his neck, dangled against his broad, bronze chest, while at his left knee hung a rattle made of deer's hoofs.

Among the more elderly Indians there was less display in dress, but many of the young women were in holiday raiment, adding a still further touch of color to the picture. Among the latter was Gentle Maiden, the daughter of Captain Pipe. A loose gown of doeskin worked with many colored beads and the quills of porcupines hung from her shoulders to her ankles. On her feet were ornamented moccasins and above them leggins. Two long strings of beads were suspended about her neck, contrasting in color with the deep black of two heavy plaits of hair, falling nearly to her waist.

The leaves of tobacco crimpled and turned to flame on the glowing, hot coals.

"Great Spirit, listen to our words. We burn this tobacco. The smoke rises to thee. We thank thee for thy great goodness in causing our mother [the earth] to bring forth her fruits. We thank thee that our supporters [corn, beans and squashes] have yielded abundantly.

"Great Spirit, our words continue to flow toward thee. Preserve us from all danger. Preserve our aged men. Preserve our mothers. Preserve our warriors. Preserve our children. May our thanks, rising with the smoke of this tobacco, be pleasing to thee."

Thus spoke Captain Pipe. Save only for the sound of his voice, the crackling of the tobacco upon the fire, and the soughing of the wind there was perfect silence in the Council House.

Only when the address was finished did there come a stir of animation among the assembled Indians. Closer to the walls, farther from the fire, which was in the center of the floor, they crowded then, while out from among them came those who were to join in the dance of Thanksgiving. There were fourteen of these, including Lone-Elk and other warriors and behind the men came Gentle Maiden and four other young women— fourteen in all.

4

Two singers seated near the center of the large room began a weird, wildly musical chant, their words telling of thanks to the Great Spirit, while in accompaniment to their voices they beat the air with rattles made of the shells of turtles.

As the singing began the dance was started and with many graceful swayings of his body, lifting his feet but little above the ground and often striking his heels upon the earth in keeping with the music's time, Lone-Elk led his followers round and round.

Unlike the dance of war, there were no violent expressions of countenance or movements of the body; no striking or attacking of imaginary foes. Every step was gentle and every motion was graceful. Thus for two or three minutes the dance continued. The assembly looked on with quiet rapture, pleased and happy.

Presently the music ceased, the dancing was discontinued and while the dancers walked slowly and more slowly in a wide circle around the fire, an old man arose and spoke. It was Neobaw, wrinkled and lean. He wore no headdress or other ornament and his clothing consisted only of moccasins, buckskin trousers and a faded red blanket which he wore over his shoulders. His coarse and tangled hair hung loosely over his ears and about his shoulders. Neohaw was a medicine-man and was both feared and respected. His words were:

"We return thanks to Heno [thunder] for his protection from reptiles and from witches and that he has given us his rain."

The old man spoke very slowly but with a show of superior learning, as if he and no other was really fit to address so important a spirit. As he resumed his seat the singing and dancing began again and for an interval continued as before.

Again, at the conclusion of the music, an aged warrior rose. His voice quavered and his body trembled with its feebleness beneath the robe of fur about his shoulders, but his eyes shone with fervor as he said: "We return thanks to Gaoh [the wind] that by his moving the air disease has been carried from us."

Then as before the music and the dance were resumed and were followed by still another short but earnest expression of thanksgiving, each part of the exercises appearing in its proper order as Lone-Elk had planned and directed, and as many of the Delawares knew of their own knowledge that the ancient custom was.

Thanksgiving to the lakes and rivers, to the sun and moon and stars, to the trees and flowers and all nature was expressed in the many brief addresses, till at last the singers' voices were hoarse and the dancers were wet with perspiration, and weary.

An address by Captain Pipe in which he once again thanked the Great Spirit for goodness to the Delawares and for all which was theirs, concluded the religious ceremonies of the Harvest Festival and slowly the Indians dispersed from the Council House. Some went away to games and some to their lodges, while others loitered in and about the village. For the women had all been listening to the speeches and watching the dancers and had yet to prepare the feast which was to follow, continuing into the night.

By himself Lone-Elk wandered from the village. Strolling down the slight descent to the edge of the lake, he took his way along the narrow strip of sand and sod of which the beach consisted and soon was out of sight. The music and dance had recalled strongly to his mind his home among the Senecas and those earlier days before he was an exile.

An audible "Ugh" came from Lone-Elk's lips and he scowled as if out of patience with himself. Turning then and leaving the water's side, he pushed through some brush to the higher bank above. On this elevation he paused, and turning about gazed carelessly over the lake. Far across its smooth surface he could see a canoe and two young men in it.

"Palefaces," he murmured and another "Ugh," this time in a tone of contempt, parted his tight-set lips. For a second or two he watched the little craft and its occupants, then strode slowly into the forest.

A straggling half circle of perhaps a mile the Seneca's feet marked in the freshly fallen leaves while he made his way indirectly toward the village. As he drew near his listless step quickened and his reflective, downcast eyes became alert and sharp. Harsh tones were rising from a group of braves not far from him. Then his approach was noticed.

A young Delaware with only a fringed kilt and leggins covering his nakedness, turned and pointed a finger at the Seneca menacingly, but quickly another seized the outstretched hand and pressed it down. By this time the approaching Indian was close at hand.

"Does Lone-Elk know of Big Buffalo?" the foremost of the Delawares inquired. "The Seneca left the village to walk beside the water. Now he comes back from a different direction. Does he know of Big Buffalo? Know that Big Buffalo is dead in the bushes that the water runs among? Little Wolf is here. Little Wolf saw Big Buffalo dead—found the Buffalo dead among the bushes by the water—found Big Buffalo killed."

CHAPTER II – A SENTENCE OF DEATH – ACCUSED OF WITCHCRAFT

"Big Buffalo would have nothing to do with the Harvest Festival as Lone-Elk planned it and the Seneca has killed him," was in substance the report which quickly passed among the Delawares when Little Wolf had come running to the village, telling of the discovery he had made – telling how he had found the dead body among the brush and reeds as he went in search of an arrow idly sent flying from his bow, after the exercises in the Council House were over.

The finger pointed at him as he had come up, though hastily pushed aside, was enough to tell Lone-Elk that he was suspected, even if no word had been spoken.

"Is it said that Lone-Elk killed Big Buffalo?" the Seneca demanded of the Indian who told to him the news.

"Big Buffalo would not come into the Council House for the Harvest Thanksgiving that was planned by Lone-Elk," said another of the Delawares. "It is this that they say."

The scowl on the Seneca's face became more bitter and contemptuous. With a look of disdain he left the group, fast increasing in numbers about him, and walked with head held high directly to the lodge of Captain Pipe.

The finding of Big Buffalo dead had put a sudden damper on the day's festivities. The squaws discontinued their preparations for the feast, and while the young bucks and warriors gathered about to discuss the mysterious death of one of the best known, though by no means best liked, of their number, children clung about their mothers' knees as the latter also flocked from lodge to lodge to talk of the strange discovery.

There were few outward signs of excitement or emotion, – that was a thing the Indians rarely showed. But in a cold, impassive way every person in the village was keenly interested. Never had there been so disturbing a thing at a time of festivity before.

Many eyes turned toward Lone-Elk as he strode toward Captain Pipe's lodge and entered the hut. Even as he did so two warriors, still in holiday garb, came carrying the body of Big Buffalo between them. Without a word they bore the corpse to the home it had always known in life, where lived the dead man's mother — an old, old woman now, who loudly lamented the death of her son as she sat on the ground just within the tumble-down bark lodge.

"Big Buffalo is found dead," said Lone-Elk to Captain Pipe.

A look and significant shrug of the shoulders was the only answer.

"If one dies when a festival is prepared, the custom is to put the body by, — to say to the sorrowful, 'We will mourn with you another time; join in the feasting with us till the festival is over.' It is an old, old custom," Lone-Elk said. "When the festival is over, also, it may be asked, 'How did Big Buffalo die?'"

"The custom is to kill him who kills another without the right of war and not in fair fight. It is a good custom," Captain Pipe made answer and looked at the Seneca searchingly.

"Lone-Elk did not kill Big Buffalo," the younger Indian said in answer to the chief's questioning look, and his voice was icy cold.

"If Lone-Elk did not kill Big Buffalo," Captain Pipe returned in the same manner, slowly and sternly, "then shall Lone-Elk find him that did kill Big Buffalo. Let him come not back until he has done this. The Delawares have no fear of any living creature; but no Delaware kills one of his own people. With the Senecas it is not always so."

For a moment Lone-Elk's sharp eyes scrutinized the chief's face as if he would find a double meaning in the Delaware's closing sentence. Could it be that Captain Pipe knew his whole history — knew the reason he returned no more to his own nation? But quickly he answered the older Indian's scathing words, and his voice was harsh and bitter as he said:

9

"Does Captain Pipe think, then, that because Big Buffalo, like a whipped dog, slunk away and would not appear in the Festival of the Harvest, the mind of Lone-Elk was poisoned against him? In his own breast does Captain Pipe find lodgment for the thought that so petty a thing could turn a Seneca to anger? No! Hear me! Lone-Elk but smiled at the childishness of Big Buffalo."

"Let Lone-Elk show the Delawares how Big Buffalo died," the chief haughtily answered, and his tones were a challenge. Even as he spoke, too, he turned his back to the Seneca and the latter, clenching his teeth to suppress the angry words he thought, wheeled about and left the lodge.

As Lone-Elk walked quickly to his own lodge he plainly noticed that not a friendly eye was turned toward him. His own glances the Delawares evaded by looking the other way, but he knew full well that they turned to gaze after him when he had passed, and he felt the things they were saying of him. It was a desperate situation. The charge of murder might quickly be followed by the charge of witchcraft, and that could mean only a choice between flight and death.

Indeed, to hoodwink the Delawares long enough to permit him to get away from them never to return seemed to the Seneca for the moment his wisest course. Still, how had Big Buffalo died? If his death was from natural causes could he not quickly prove such to have been the case, and then, the Delawares admitting it, rebuke them for their suspicions? That would be excellent! Nothing could help him more in his keen desire for a recognized position of permanent leadership.

All in a twinkling these thoughts crowded upon the brain of Lone-Elk. They restored his great self-confidence and his feeling of superiority. Looking neither to right nor left, he walked with all the dignity of his haughty nature to the hut where the body of the dead Indian lay. With a few soothing words to the lamenting squaws about the door, he entered the rude shelter and bent low over the silent figure of the departed warrior. Even as he did so a new thought came to the Seneca and he gloomily shrugged his shoulders as if to conceal his delight from those who might be watching.

Slowly Lone-Elk examined the half-covered body of Big Buffalo and silently nodded his head as if he found only that which he expected to find.

"See," he said very calmly to the women and to Fishing Bird and one or two other braves who had drawn near,—"see, no bruises. A witch has killed Big Buffalo. It is as Lone-Elk says. Only a witch's power can kill a warrior so."

"A witch—Big Buffalo killed by a witch!" The word was spread about the village with the speed of the wind.

Many of the Indians and Captain Pipe among them gathered about the Seneca.

"It is as Lone-Elk supposed. It is as Lone-Elk now says; a witch has killed Big Buffalo," he boldly declared. "Listen to my words. Lone-Elk knows the hand which struck a warrior of the Delawares down. Lone-Elk alone can tell how Big Buffalo died; but the Delawares well know the custom of the people of the Long House [the Iroquois] and of all the Indians, that witches shall be put to death."

There was a stir of ill-suppressed excitement. Lone-Elk was using strong words. Whom would he accuse? To be accused of practicing witchcraft was nothing short of a sentence of death. The accusation was itself sufficient. No evidence was necessary.

"Lone-Elk knows the hand which reached out to wither the strength of Big Buffalo, even as flowers are turned black by cold," the Seneca went on, slowly and solemnly. "When the speeches and the dancing in the Council House were over Lone-Elk walked to cool himself beside the water. Across the lake he saw in a canoe the young Palefaces who have come unbidden here to cut down the trees and drive off the game which belong only to the Indians,—even as others of the Longknives have done in the lands where

11

lived our fathers. Two of the Palefaces there were when Lone-Elk first saw them.

"Again Lone-Elk looked and only one was there—only one Paleface in the canoe; but over the water floated a cloud of foul-smelling vapor. Nearer and nearer the cloud came. Soon it passed into the woods. Again did Lone-Elk look. Again the cloud appeared and as it moved across the quiet waters drew near the canoe in which there still was but one of the two Palefaces.

"And even as Lone-Elk watched a strange thing happened. Quick as the leap of a frightened deer was the cloud changed to the form of a bird—a large, black bird with heavy, beating wings. Straight to the canoe the great bird flew. Still Lone-Elk watched closely and held his breath hard with wonder. Once, twice the strange bird circled about the solitary Paleface, then flew swiftly into the canoe. Instantly there appeared two young Palefaces where only one had been before. And the bird,—the big, black bird was gone. In his hands the Paleface witch—he you call 'Little Paleface' it is—held a tomahawk.

"The sun shone bright upon it and even far across the water did Lone-Elk see the red blood still wet and shining. Not then did Lone-Elk know. Not then did Lone-Elk guess the awful thing which happened. Now does he know—now do all the Delawares know how came Big Buffalo to die."

There was a stir followed by a deeply threatening murmur among the assembled Indians. It boded ill—ah, ill indeed,—to the young white pioneers.

Flushed with the success of his narrative and vain to find himself so hearkened to, even by those who a little while before were his accusers, the Seneca would have added to his extraordinary story and elaborated upon the many fearsome shapes the cloud assumed of which he told. The words were in his mind but he hesitated to try the credulity of the Delawares further. Yet speak he must. The Indians still pressed nearer. They would hear more; and Lone-Elk therefore continued.

"The witch must die. If only one Paleface is bewitched then only one must die. Let all the Delawares hear now and remember. Lone-Elk will kill him that killed Big Buffalo — and the White Fox as well, if the White Fox is also a witch as his brother that you call 'Little Pale-face' is."

If any of the Indians doubted the words of the Seneca, none showed it. Few red men there were who did not believe in witchcraft and Lone-Elk had made his tale just fanciful and weird enough to win and hold their faith in all his declarations.

In those days too, not only among the Delawares but among more advanced Indian nations as well, witchcraft was more than a mere superstition. It was feared and hated as an actually existing thing, more awful than the most deadly disease. The declaration of any one Indian that another was a witch was almost certain to be followed by the killing of the one accused. It was the duty as well as the privilege of the accuser to take the other's life.

Little wonder is it, when these circumstances are considered, that Lone-Elk's declarations, made in the most convincing and emphatic manner of which his eloquence was capable, made a deep impression! Many were visibly frightened. The thought that soon they might be struck down, even as Big Buffalo had been, was far more disquieting than to face a foe in hand-to-hand combat.

One of the Delawares there was, however, who went quietly away soon after Lone-Elk had finished speaking, and as if only loitering about, came presently to his own hut. Here he removed the gayest part of the holiday dress he wore, including the sash of scarlet cloth — relic of some plundered settlement, no doubt — and with his gun over his shoulder sauntered again through the village as if he were starting out to hunt.

This Indian was Fishing Bird. He found Lone-Elk still talking, — still surrounded by an attentive, awestruck throng. When the Harvest Festival was over, the Seneca was saying, then would be the time to mourn Big Buffalo's death and then the time to avenge his murder. It was an old, old custom, he went on, that if one died when a festival was being enjoyed, the body should be laid aside until the season of the merrymaking was over. Addressing Captain Pipe directly, he appealed to the chief to say if the ancient custom should not now be observed.

The leader of the Delawares saw plainly that Lone-Elk's proposal pleased his people.

"Then shall it be as the Seneca says," he made answer, and waiting to hear nothing more, Fishing Bird, with a glance across the lake to make certain the white boys were still fishing near the far-away shore, turned slowly into the woods. He walked with lagging steps only until the village was left well behind, then eagerly dashed forward at a run.

CHAPTER III — THE WARNING

"Now just-one more!"

"Oh, look a'here! that's what you've been saying for a half hour or more! You see where the sun is, don't you!"

"All right, then, I don't care; but there's-a regular whale almost on my hook and it's too bad to-disappoint him," the first speaker returned. Even as he answered, however, he drew in the long, heavy fishing pole he held and followed his companion's example in winding his line on a broad, flat stick notched at both ends.

It was time, indeed, that the day's sport be ended. The autumn sun was scarcely visible through the branches of the trees to the west. The air, so soft and warm at mid-day, was growing cold, and six miles or more lay between the young fishermen and the homely but snug log cabin which was their home, and whose pleasant fire and comforts the nipping wind now made doubly attractive.

Those of you who have read "Far Past the Frontier" or "Connecticut Boys in the Western Reserve" will have recognized in the two fisher lads thus introduced Return Kingdom and John Jerome, once more in the Ohio wilderness to complete their home-making after the trying times of the preceding spring and winter, ending, as you know, with the recovery of the hidden fortune which cost so many lives and for which so many searched in vain.

Of course it was John, — slight of figure but strong, tough and wiry as a wolf, and full of fun as a lively young fellow of eighteen or so could be, who had shown such reluctance to put away his line and yield no longer to the temptation to try for "just one more."

Of course it was Ree Kingdom, tall and broad shouldered, who pointed out the fast-setting sun and recognized the necessity of starting homeward before darkness hid the way. Somehow it always was left to Ree to guide and direct. His quiet manner, energy, resourcefulness and thoughtfulness

15

made him naturally the leader. He was very little older than his lifelong friend, Jerome, but the latter was always willing that Ree should be the captain in all their various enterprises. And yet it may well be said that John was a very agreeable and helpful private in all undertakings, whether in matters of work, matters of sport and recreation, or matters involving their common safety in this wild country of Ohio where they had set about to establish their home and at the same time carry on a profitable trade with the Indians.

"We might have crossed over and had a look at the Delawares' Harvest Festival," said John, stretching himself preparatory to beginning the homeward journey.

"Still, the art of minding your own business is often worth cultivating. It's a pretty good idea, sometimes," Kingdom answered with a smile, and picked up a paddle to shove the canoe off into deeper water. Just as he did so a piece of dried mud, such as would weigh an ounce or two, dropped into the little craft directly in front of him.

"Hello, here! Hello, Fishing Bird!" exclaimed John who, as he was facing the reed-lined shore, was the first to see whence the bit of dried earth came, and recognized at once an old friend from the Indian town.

"How now, Fishing Bird? We thought you were busy with the Harvest Festival that Lone-Elk planned so grandly. How come—"

Kingdom's greeting, rapidly following John's, was interrupted by the Indian placing a finger to his lips and shaking his head most earnestly.

"Paleface brothers listen, Paleface brothers not make any noise at all. Hear all Fishing Bird will say," the Delaware began in a subdued undertone, keeping himself almost wholly concealed by the tall grass and reeds at the water's edge.

"No! look other way!" he urged, speaking rapidly but low, as both the white lads turned toward him. "Maybe Lone-Elk watching. Lone-Elk says Little Paleface is a witch and must be killed. Big Buffalo is dead—found dead by Little Wolf in the bushes by the water—and now Lone-Elk says a cloud that was Little Paleface bewitched touched Big Buffalo with a tomahawk and so he died. So must Little Paleface go away—go far, heap far away. Go soon—right now! Lone-Elk come quick. Bye."

A slight rustling of the grass was followed by silence. For a second the young white men waited, their faces turned away from the shore as the Indian had asked. When they no longer heard him, however, they quickly looked about, but only to find themselves alone. As quietly as he had come and as suddenly, had the Delaware disappeared.

Considerably perplexed and more than a little astonished, the boys looked at each other inquiringly.

"Real nice," said John. "It appears that I'm a witch and that I touched Big Buffalo with a tomahawk and killed him! What d'ye think of that, now!"

A smile which was more brave than merry was on John's face, but Ree's brow was wrinkled by deep thought.

"There's a chance that Fishing Bird has stretched this thing—that it's not half as bad as he makes out," Kingdom returned at last. "But the worst of it is, we don't know. Hang it all, why did he have to rush off so after telling just enough to make us want to know more? Yet we've got to give him credit for what he has done, and the only safe thing is to take full account of all he said,—take full account of all of it till we find out just what it's worth, at least."

"What d'ye say to going across to their town and finding out just what that Seneca's up to, Ree? Pretend, of course, that we haven't heard a thing unusual; just dropped in to look at the Festival and say 'howdy.'"

But Kingdom shook his head to this proposal at once.

"If there's going to be trouble it will catch us soon enough without our setting out to hunt it," he said. "Fishing Bird was in dead earnest and afraid lest he be caught or suspected of giving warning. That's the reason he left so quickly. No, John, the thing for us to do is to make tracks in good order toward the little log house and keep our eyes open every minute."

"And I killed Big Buffalo—just to think that I killed that ugly, prowling, malicious old rascal! Faith, 'twould make me laugh if—if—"

John's musing exclamation was unfinished. With a swift stroke of the paddle Kingdom sent the canoe sweeping through the water with sudden liveliness and the lad who, under the name of "Little Paleface," must answer to the charge of witchcraft, could only seize a paddle, also, to use as a rudder and likewise assist in hurrying the light bark craft onward.

Heading into a long arm of the lake extending northward, the boys touched shore at last at a little point of high ground which projected through the mass of rank grass, reeds and bushes bordering the water at this point, and continued on foot among trees and underbrush. Kingdom shouldered the canoe while John carried their rifle, paddles and goodly string of fish.

There was not much opportunity to talk and each lad was busy with his own thoughts. However, when after a long walk overland they reached a considerable' stream, by the aid of which they could complete their journey in the more comfortable manner the canoe afforded them, John was not long in breaking the silence.

"Ree," he said, with rather more earnestness and show of temper than was usual with him, "I shouldn't be surprised if they come for me tonight. Confound the ignorant beasts!"

"I've been thinking so," was the answer, "and I'm afraid they will."

"The cabin ain't in as good shape as it used to be; the logs dry and the roof drier! And honest to goodness, Ree, I don't see what we're going to do about it; I can't help but feel but that I'm to blame for the mess, somehow, though what I ever did to get Lone-Elk down on me I don't know, blamed if I do!"

"Why, you're nothing of the kind, John! Get all such foolishness out of your head. And what we're going to do about it is to be ready for them! I guess we can take care of ourselves now that we know what's likely to happen. Actually, the thing that bothers me most is just the thought of where we'd have landed but for Fishing Bird letting us know. If ever there was an all white heart in a red skin, it's his, and there's no doubt about it."

"And tomorrow we will find out from some one from the village or other Indians that happen to pass, just how the land lays — that is, if — if we don't find out sooner," John replied with a grim smile. "And Big Buffalo's dead! I can hardly believe it, by thunder! I guess it was the Seneca that killed him, if anybody did. Don't you s'pose Lone-Elk killed him, Ree?"

"Can't tell. Off-hand I'd say it couldn't have been any one else. It's been common talk this long while that Lone-Elk and Big Buffalo didn't hitch up worth a hill o' beans, but — and hang it all, it's this that makes the whole thing so bad a mess — we simply don't know."

This phase of the curious situation in which they found themselves — this air of mystery and uncertainty connected with the report and warning which had reached them, afforded a more fertile subject for discussion by the two boys than did the question of their own personal safety. The latter was a matter which must await developments, and neither boy yet realized how serious the situation was. Their quickly made agreement to hold the fort and face the trouble bravely had, for the time, disposed of that question.

But the death of the Delaware who had always been so hostile to them, and the mysterious trick of fate by which, though dead, he was still the direct cause of trouble coming just when all their plans were going forward so smoothly, and just when they were in every way getting along so comfortably, gave occasion for much speculation and exchange of ideas.

"It's not so hard to understand why Lone-Elk should want to get rid of us and to make trouble for us," said Kingdom reflectively, "because all summer he has been talking war and stirring things up generally."

19

"And even hinting that we were sending word of what all the Delawares were doing straight to Mad Anthony at Fort Pitt," John broke in warmly. "Fishing Bird it was that told us that, too."

"Still I'd like to know just what took Big Buffalo off his pins," was Ree's reply, and so the conversation continued with no conclusion being reached excepting only that there was going to be trouble and it must be met and faced just as it had been confronted and finally overcome so many times before.

It may have been, indeed, most likely was, the very fact that always in the past they had come out of the most perilous difficulties without permanent injury, which made the two boys slow to appreciate the gravity of their present position—a position of the greatest danger; far from all human assistance and with all the Indians who hitherto had been their friends now turned against them.

The little house of logs perched on the eastern bluff directly above the river would no doubt have seemed a very lonesome spot and insecure enough to other eyes, as the boys approached it in the autumn twilight, but not so to them. With its surroundings of small but well cultivated fields in the valley below, its big, comfortable looking woodpile at the edge of the woods and the cheerful welcome of Neb and Phoebe, their two horses, whinnying their greeting from the rude log stable, it was a pleasure to them to be safely there once more.

It was home. The stout log walls would soon shut out the darkness and, they believed, the danger, holding them snug and warm with the firelight and the pleasant smell of their cooking supper within.

John looked after the horses at the barn while Kingdom built up the fire in the cabin and soon had the fish deliciously frying and several extremely generous slices of coarse corn bread toasting on the hearth. A pot of maple tea—(maple sugar boiled in water—an Indian drink) simmered from its hook above the blaze, and a bark tray of nuts, cracked and ready for dessert, was in waiting on the table.

"Better have everything shut tight," suggested Ree as John came in.

"That's what I've done," was the answer, "not a knot-hole open. But — well, now that we are home and so jolly comfortable, does it not seem to you just as if Fishing Bird's coming and all that he said was just some nasty dream and not really so at all? Does to me. I don't forget it for more than a minute at a time, but I feel as if I'd wake up pretty soon and find I'd just been sleeping on my back."

"Well, it's too bad," was the answer.

"We've got too much else to do to be bothered this way," John returned.

"I've been thinking," Ree went on, "that Captain Pipe may give that Seneca to understand a thing or two and prove to be our friend again, just when we most need him, as he has done more than once before. Still we've got to look alive every minute till the trouble's over, and so you put the supper on the table, John, and I'll just take a little look around the house and cast my eyes about the clearing for a minute."

CHAPTER IV — WATCHED

"Peaceful as a Nanny goat," was Kingdom's declaration upon returning from his scouting expedition a quarter of an hour later, and both boys sat down to their evening meal feeling for the time quite secure. As was natural, however, their conversation still centered upon the strange news and warning which had come to them and they discussed many plans of possible action.

One thing seemed apparent; they must remain near the cabin or the Indians, finding it empty, would be very likely, under Lone-Elk's leadership, to destroy it. Except to stay where they were, therefore, and face the Seneca and his charges, only one course was open. This was to take their horses and such goods as could be carried, and seek the protection of Fort Pitt or Gen. Wayne's army encamped near there.

Of the whole evening's talk, however, but one thing, in addition to the plan argued at the very first, was settled. It was that John should be in readiness to make his escape if such a move were found necessary. It was he and he alone who was charged with witchcraft. Fishing Bird had made this plain. Ree would be in danger only as the friend of the "witch" and it was unlikely, considering the friendly relations the boys had always sought to maintain with the Delawares, that harm would come to the elder lad unless some specific charge were lodged against him, or unless he should be forced into the fight in defense of his friend.

The latter situation was what Ree himself fully expected. If there was to be trouble he would court his full share of it and he would not have thought of planning otherwise.

Soon after supper the boys covered their fire with ashes, making the interior of the cabin completely dark; and though they spent the succeeding hours in conversation they watched the surrounding clearing from the loopholes.

Neither had much desire to sleep, but at last John prevailed upon Kingdom to lie down for awhile, and he alone remained on guard until nearly morning. Once he was given a lively thrill when a dark object emerged slowly and cautiously from the woods and crept toward the cabin. But the visitor proved to be only a wolf, which presently trotted away and was lost in the shadows again, and Jerome was well pleased that he had given Kingdom no chance to laugh by taking alarm when no danger threatened.

Some time before daybreak, Ree, who had slept but little, arose and ordered John to bed. The latter reluctantly obeyed. "For," he said, "if a surprise is what the Seneca has in mind, it will be just before morning that they'll be most likely to come."

But the long night passed without a disturbing sound. When Jerome bounced out of his bunk of blankets spread upon freshly gathered leaves, after troubled dreams in which Big Buffalo pursued him with an upraised hatchet resembling a gorgeously colored sunset cloud, it was to find a cheerful blaze in the fireplace and Ree washing up the dishes left untouched since supper. The door stood open and the cool, pure air with its scent of frost-nipped leaves was like a tonic. The tinkle of the water along the banks of the river below rose musically in the almost perfect quiet prevailing in both the woods and clearing, and nowhere was there hint or sign that danger lurked near and nearer.

Waiting—lingering over their breakfast, glancing often and anxiously through the open door and frequently going out to scan the clearing from side to side and from end to end—waiting, they hardly knew for what,—in the early morning the young settlers began to find time hanging heavily on their hands.

They were not accustomed to such inactivity. To feel compelled to remain idle, too, when there were so many things they wished to be doing, was almost as trying as it was to bear up cheerfully under the constant thought that the next hour,—the next minute, even—might find them fighting for their very lives.

"This certainly seems like a lot of foolishness," said John, at last impatiently.

"But seeming and being are two altogether different things," Ree answered. "Still, it's not very comfortable or enjoyable, I'll admit. But what else can we be doing?"

"Some one's coming!" exclaimed John in an undertone, instantly changing the trend of both his own thoughts and Ree's. He was standing out where he could command a view of the river, while Kingdom sat in the doorway.

Quietly and with an appearance of unconcern Ree rose and went forward. Looking in the direction John in a whisper indicated, he saw three half-naked savages two hundred yards or more up the stream. They were hastily dragging a canoe out of the water and up onto the bank opposite that on which the cabin stood.

"Holler at them! Sing out something!" John urged, looking toward the Indians again himself. Not to attract their notice he had at first pretended he did not see them. "Blest if I know any of them!" he added, looking more closely.

Already the redskins were well up on the river bank and two of them had lifted the canoe up to their shoulders.

"I can't make out why they are leaving the water in that way," Ree answered. "Maybe we can find out. Ho, there! Howdy, brothers!"

Kingdom's voice was clear and strong. There could be no doubt of the Indians having heard him, but the only effect of his words, apparently, was to send them hurrying into the woods the faster and in another second they had disappeared from sight.

"Umph!" Kingdom ejaculated wonderingly, "I believe they're afraid of you, John,—afraid to sail down past us! But you can't tell much about it, either. It may be they thought they'd find us gone and were taken by surprise to find out otherwise."

"Well, it shows one thing, we never saw such a queer piece of business before, and it simply proves that there's something wrong and most likely it's just what Fishing Bird told us," John answered, pretty soberly.

"Yes, it proves that there's something up, sure, and I guess we're both tired of waiting to find out more about it," said Kingdom decisively. "So I'll tell you what we'll do: Just you keep yourself safe somewhere and I'll ride Phoebe over to the Delaware town and find out all about it. We'll surely get no news, good or bad, from Indians happening to go by if they all break into the woods on the far side of the river, before getting here!"

"Ree, you've told me a thousand times, if you've told me once, to be prudent. Now how about being prudent yourself? We'd better wait! We'll get some word, yet."

Kingdom made no answer at once, but he was still thinking of the plan he had so impulsively proposed and the more he pondered the more it appealed to him. Then he began to give John the benefit of his thoughts — began to argue that they could not afford to wait indefinitely, with only their supposition that they would be attacked as a reason; began to point out that the time to win the favorable attention of Captain Pipe was before fighting took place, not afterward; began to regret that he had not gone to the town of the Delawares earlier. But he would not admit that he himself would be in danger, though ever so anxious lest John should not properly take care of himself in his absence.

As usual, Kingdom had his way, though in this case it might well be questioned whether his was the right way, all things considered, and especially in view of what happened afterward.

With a final word of caution to John to keep himself safe by staying within easy reach of the cabin's thick walls, Kingdom mounted the docile mare, given them by Theodore Hatch, the Quaker, and set off at a gallop. It was a delightfully warm, sunny autumn day and but for the load upon his spirits the daring young rider, dashing in and out among the trees, where the rough trail crooked and curved, would have been buoyantly happy. The

25

ground was carpeted with freshly fallen leaves. The foliage of the underbrush was still scarcely touched by the frost, and the cawing of the crows and chatter of numerous smaller birds imparted a feeling as if life were a long, bright holiday.

Still, Ree could not rid his mind of the sense of danger which, like a shadow, followed always closely with him, and he turned over and over in his thoughts plan after plan for laying the whole cause of his visit clearly before Captain Pipe, and asking his interference.

Fresh and active, Phoebe kept a steady, rapid gallop, wherever the overhanging branches would permit such speed, and in but little more than an hour Kingdom drew rein within a short walk of the Indian town.

It was Ree's intention to ascertain as fully as possible just what the Delawares were doing, and then, if the situation were not too serious, ride up to and among the scattered collection of huts as boldly and freely as he would have done on any other occasion.

But his pause to reconnoiter was fortunate. He had left the portage trail, an extension of which led to the village, and sheltered himself among some small, low trees thickly growing between the path and the lake. Dismounting, he listened closely but heard no sound. Even the Indian town must be very quiet, he thought, that not so much as a voice or the bark of a dog was heard. However, he slipped the bridle rein over Phoebe's head and hung it loosely upon a short, projecting branch, preparatory to going forward to investigate on foot.

A footstep, light as a feather, but instantly caught by his quick ear, made Ree start. Over his shoulder he saw, half hidden by some bushes, a face turned toward him and a hand upraised in a way commanding silence.

"Gentle Maiden!" He spoke the name in an undertone, which showed both his surprise and his friendly feeling for the one addressed.

"I heard the hoofs of your horse," said the Indian girl, drawing stealthily nearer and in the same manner looking all about her. "My Paleface brother's friend—he is not here." Her words seemed to put a question she feared to more directly ask, and Kingdom realized at once, if he had ever doubted before, that the warning from Fishing Bird was not without most serious reason.

While the young white man hesitated to speak, not knowing just how much he dared let the daughter of Captain Pipe understand that he knew, she continued:

"My Paleface brother is in danger. Big Buffalo was found dead and Lone-Elk, the stranger from afar, has said a witch has done it—killed Big Buffalo with a witch's hatchet that leaves no mark. Lone-Elk says the witch is Little Paleface, the friend of my brother here,—says he saw Little Paleface, bewitched, strike the Delaware down. Even now have Lone-Elk and some others gone to seize him."

"And Captain Pipe, your father—does Captain Pipe let them do this?" Ree asked, trying to remain calm.

"The custom is that the witch must die," the girl made answer, turning her eyes away.

"Gentle Maiden, you know that John Jerome—you know that Little Paleface is no witch; that he no more killed Big Buffalo than you did." Kingdom's voice was half angry in its impatient earnestness.

"The customs of the Indians are not the customs of the white people," the girl made answer. "Lone-Elk is powerful. What Gentle Maiden believes would be as dipping water from the lake yonder with a cup—making no difference one way, no difference another."

"But Captain-Pipe knows better, Gentle Maiden."

"Hopocon—my father, that you call Captain Pipe—wants none of the Paleface teachings. When the missionaries told Gentle Maiden long ago there were no witches, he only pitied them that they knew no better."

"But—"

"No, no!" the girl broke out hurriedly. "My Paleface brother must not wait talking here. That which is, must be. Not long has Lone-Elk been gone. By riding fast the White Fox can reach his cabin before the coming of the Seneca, and with Little Paleface soon be far away where Lone-Elk will not find them. Haste! Gentle Maiden has done all she can. Paleface brother must not remember who has told him this, but oh, he must remember what he has heard! Hurry, hurry, now, or—"

"I'll go, Gentle Maiden, I'll go. If I can ever pay back the kindness you have done both John and me, I'll not be slow to do it, you may be sure. But it's a downright shame—no, what I mean is that you need never fear anyone will so much as suspect that you told me this or anything. Good-bye, good-bye."

With such feverish anxiety and haste did Ree speak, now that he was bent only on flying to John's rescue, he scarce knew what he said; but in a trice he was in the saddle. And yet quickly as he moved, when he turned to give a parting nod the Indian girl was gone.

Long familiarity with the woods had made the beautiful, intelligent mare, Phoebe, almost as free and light-footed among the trees and brush and rough ground, often broken by rougher roots and fallen branches, as a deer. Kingdom placed all dependence in his horse's ability to avoid or clear every obstruction and urged the gentle creature to the utmost, paying little heed to anything save to escape the limbs of trees overhead as he hastened on. He had at once concluded that Lone-Elk and his band were undoubtedly traveling toward the cabin by the route to the east of the lake and the swamp which bounded a considerable portion of it, for otherwise he must have met them. He knew that they could easily have heard him approaching and hidden themselves until he passed, but long training had made his ears sharp and his eyes the same. Maybe he had this time, however, placed too much dependence in them.

"Anyhow, we'll soon know, my pet," he murmured with teeth clenched, and Phoebe seemed to understand.

Out upon the bluffs above the river, into the open for a moment, then down the precipitous hills and across the water at a shallow place horse and rider went, and, emerging soon from the woods again, were in the natural clearing—the clearing which had originally tempted the boy pioneers to locate here.

All was quiet. The cabin stood like a sentry at rest on the high bank rising abruptly from the river, then sloping down on all sides away from it. The yellow, autumn sunlight made the whole scene appear even drowsily tranquil. A sense of relief came to Kingdom, and he even felt chagrined that he had been so decidedly disturbed.

Still it was strange that John did not show himself. Perhaps the exceeding quiet all about was, after all, fraught with greatest danger. Perhaps—but Ree was at the foot of the slope now and his mind had scarcely time to present another thought before he was up the hill, and throwing himself from the horse, quickly entered the open door of the low log house.

"John!" he called in a low tone—and a little catch in his throat which he could not control, gave his voice a tremulous quaver. "John!"

"Yes, Ree;" the answer was scarcely more than a whisper, "I'm up here in the loft, and listen! You can hear me?"

"Every word."

"Don't act surprised or excited or show that you have found out or heard anything, for they're watching now—Lone-Elk and a pack of Delawares have surrounded the clearing. I've been peeking through a crack, watching 'em half an hour or more."

CHAPTER V — IN DRIPPING RAIN AND DARKNESS

With what consternation Kingdom received the startling intelligence John's words conveyed would never have been guessed from his actions. He tossed his rough, squirrel-skin cap on the bunk, which was a bed by night and a lounge by day, and sat down, wiping the perspiration from his forehead.

"They're after me, I s'pose, Ree, — blame 'em!" Jerome went on in the same half whisper. "I just happened to be up here pawing over some of the skins stored away so long, and got a glimpse of the rascals among the trees. So I've been watching ever since, and I don't want you to think I crawled up here to hide. Just so much as hint at such a thing and I'll —"

John did not say what he would do, but seeing how he hated being found in a position which might be taken as a reflection upon his courage, Ree was considerably tempted to suggest that maybe he himself had better get under the bed. But it was no time for joke-making and the facetious thought had no more than occurred to him than, unspoken, it was forgotten.

"Stay up there, John, old boy; see everything you can. I'll stroll out and put Phoebe in the lean-to and gape around some in a natural sort of way myself. The whole business looks mighty bad. What Fishing Bird said is all true; I found out that much. I'll tell you about it when I come in."

If John Jerome had been a lad easily alarmed or one likely to fall a ready victim to a too lively imagination, Return Kingdom would certainly have thought that he had done so in this case when, after unsaddling the mare and tying her in her stall, he sat down in the open doorway of the cabin and with apparent indifference scanned the clearing from end to end, without seeing the slightest sign of the Indians' presence.

With his elbow on his knee, his head upon his hand, as if he were merely resting, he continued to watch the wooded boundary most intently from between the fingers which concealed his eyes. He had little fear that the

Indians would fire upon him from some place of concealment among the trees; the distance was too great. A white hunter might easily have brought down a deer at the same number of yards with an exceptionally heavy charge in his long-barreled rifle, but the Redskins, as Ree well knew, usually loaded with so little powder, owing to its scarcity with them, no doubt, that he had little to fear in thus exposing himself so long as the enemy came no nearer than the edge of the woods.

"You're downright sure you saw them, John?" inquired Kingdom, in a low voice, rising and entering.

"There he goes! There—did you see that?" came an excited undertone from Jerome as if in answer.

Instantly Kingdom looked out but he saw nothing.

"I vow! I think it was the Seneca!" John whispered. "He ran from the big beech near the patch to the clump of little trees at the left. Guess he thought no one was watching but you, and darted out when your back was turned."

"I'll stay back out of sight a bit, and you look sharp. Maybe we can make out what they're up to," Kingdom replied. Then, to lead the savages to suppose that their presence was not suspected, Ree went about making a bright fire as if to prepare dinner, and soon the smoke from the cabin chimney conveyed to the crouching redskins in hiding along the clearing's edge the very impression he wished them to receive.

Kingdom spent half an hour,—a long half hour of suspense and anxious thoughts—in putting the room to rights, busying himself in a dozen different ways, while John peered closely from the crack, to see through which his eyes had already been strained so long they ached severely. Still he saw nothing. Whether the savages were only extremely wary or whether, as the boys fervently hoped, they had slipped away and gone as silently as they came could not be known, and continued vigilance was the only key to their safety.

All day John Jerome remained concealed in the loft, watching almost constantly from the narrow crevice which permitted him to see without being seen. All day Return Kingdom went about from the cabin into the lean-to barn, from the barn into the cabin again, and in and out of the open door a hundred times on one pretext and another, doing his best to make his every movement seem composed and natural.

He was certain in his own mind that the savages were watching for John. Perhaps they expected to see him in some fantastic and witch-like shape, — see him change from a cloud to human form, or turn himself into some wild beast.

Once a wandering crow flew into the clearing and circled idly over the little cornfield. As it flew down to a shock of corn, both boys chanced to notice it and both saw, too, a sudden, rapid movement, and then another and another, within the fringe of the woods. Were they the dancing shadows of wind-tossed branches, or were the Seneca and his band still near? Quick as the movements were, little as the boys had seen, they knew the answer to the question which occurred to them and thanked the vagrant crow for the information he had been the means of giving them.

"Still," said John, "if those fool Delawares get it into their heads that that crow is me, and like as not Lone-Elk may tell 'em some such thing, it'll just make the whole lot of them believe more than ever that I am a sure enough witch."

Full well did Kingdom realize how very correct John's observation probably was. He was confident that it was the crow which occasioned the moving about among the hiding Indians, — the flitting shadows both he and John had seen. He made no answer to his friend's remark at once, but turned over again in his mind a plan which he had been considering all day. It seemed wise. He could think of nothing better.

"John," said Ree at last, "if they stay away till it's dark enough to do it, how would you like to slip away and go up among the rocky ledges for a few days?"

"Hide?" Jerome demanded rather contemptuously.

"Why, no! There's no need to call it hiding," Kingdom answered tactfully. "Just stay away from the cabin for awhile and give me a chance to find out what killed Big Buffalo and get the witch idea out of these crazy Delawares' minds."

"But, don't you—"

"I know what you're going to say. It is, don't I think that the fact of your being away will make the Indians all the more certain about this witchcraft business—make them think you've skedaddled! We can't help what they think. We do know, though, that they're after you and either we've got to pack up and light out, or get this witch idea out of their heads. Now I think I can do it, in spite of Gentle Maiden's discouraging talk; if I only have a chance."

On one point, as the discussion continued, hardly above a whisper, both boys agreed. It was that some time during the night the Indians would visit the cabin. They might come as if in a friendly way just to learn whether Little Paleface was there; or they might make a determined attack. The redskins' supposition that Ree was alone, confirmed by all that they had seen during the day, however, would probably suggest to them an apparently friendly, but in reality spying, visit.

In whatever way the lads viewed their situation they found so much of uncertainty surrounding them that at best they must take a chance.

Often and often was it this way in pioneer days. Every important movement was encompassed by more or less danger. If a settler needed but to go to mill, or to some frontier trading place for supplies, he confronted many uncertainties and often left his family in danger, too. Danger was always present, and although only the foolhardy were disregardful entirely, even the most prudent came by constant association to take it as a matter of course.

33

The latter was the feeling of the two boys from Connecticut. If they had been less accustomed to the alarms of the wilderness, they would, in the pinch in which they now found themselves, most probably have sought safety at once at Fort Pitt or perhaps at some of the Ohio river settlements. If they had done so their story would have been a very different one.

Though he had but reluctantly agreed to Ree's proposal, not wishing to leave his friend to face the situation alone, John found so much to think about in the prospect of spending the night—and it might be many nights and days—alone in the woods, that the reflection that he also would be in danger was almost comforting. He thought with dread of the long and lonely hours of darkness without even a camp-fire's comfort, but somehow there was something quite interesting about it all, too. Perhaps it was the change and the excitement, as he planned how stealthily he would steal through the woods, that appealed to him. Certain it is that he found himself anxious to be gone, and watching the deepening shadows almost impatiently lest something happen to prevent his departure before thick darkness came. His greatest fear lay in the fact that on three sides at least the cabin was, in all probability, still surrounded by Indians. On the fourth or west side was the river. How was he to reach the open woods? How reach the rocky ledges to the north and east, among whose deep ravines and clefts and long, narrow passages and shallow caves he would remain until the rage of the savages had passed?

A bank of clouds, wide as the eye could see above the treetops, had come up out of the southwest to meet the sinking sun and, when at last the shadows had filled the valley, darkness came on rapidly. The wind rose, too, and quite before its approach was suspected, a drizzling fall rain had set in, which gave promise of continuing all night.

The cabin door had stood open all day, but Ree felt he could close it now without exciting the suspicions of those who watched. As he did so, John clambered quickly down from the low loft and slipped noiselessly through the low opening connecting the lean-to stable and the single room of the cabin itself. How well he remembered the good purpose the hole had served once before! He remarked to Ree about it with a nervous little laugh, recalling that lively battle of their early days in the woods and how nearly fatal to them both it had been. But Kingdom told him to make haste; that they could not know who was watching now, and in the darkness there might be Indians even within hearing of a whisper.

Ree had improved the opportunity before night came on to fill John's powder horn and bullet pouch and to pack in the form of a knapsack for him a blanket and a supply of dried meat and bread. These, with Jerome's rifle, he had previously passed through the "cat hole," as it was called, into the stable; but now that John had followed them, he suddenly found himself wishing that he had planned otherwise. Yet confident all was for the best, though the wind never had had so much of awful homesickness in its mournful sounds before, though the rain never before had beaten with such seeming tearful sorrow upon the roof, he whispered hastily:

"Be careful, old boy. Look for news by the day after tomorrow if you hear nothing before, and be sure that everything will be all right in a few days at most."

"And you come where I am the minute you're in danger, mind," John answered. "Good-bye, Ree, I'm going along the river's edge. It'll be easy to get past anybody or anything tonight. Good-bye."

Ree would have whispered another word of caution and of farewell, but he realized that John was gone — felt it in his very bones that he was alone, alone; and the autumn wind blew more mournfully than ever; the patter of the raindrops sounded twice as melancholy as before.

For many minutes Kingdom intently listened, then throwing wide the cabin door, made a pretense of emptying just beyond the doorstep the wooden, trough-like bowl which did duty as a wash basin. Though he made a brave show of unconcern, his heart beat hard and fast. But he was glad to see how totally dark the night was. One must have been very close indeed if he had seen John emerge from the darkness of the lean-to into the equal blackness without, he thought. Surely the Indians, if still watching, would never suspect him going out that way, and not having seen him at all would be very certain that he had been gone for a full day at least, should they call at the cabin and still not discover him.

Despite the storm, the night was warm for so late in the season, and Kingdom was glad to have the door ajar while he waited for the first step which would tell him of the Indians' coming. He had no doubt they would come, unless their general plan was quite different from what he supposed it to be. Still, time dragged on bringing no tidings — no sound but the drip, drip of the rain, the sad sighing of the wind and now and then the rattle of some loose puncheon on the roof, moved by a passing gust more lively than the rest.

Again and again Ree mentally computed the distance John had probably traveled in the time that he had been gone. "Now he must be just about at the foot of the bluff and creeping along the water's edge, shielded by the higher bank of the river," he thought at first. "Now he must be half-way to the woods. Now, if nothing has happened, he is past the worst of the danger and safe among the trees."

And so thinking, encouraged by the absence of any alarming sound, Kingdom breathed easier, and was glad John had gone along the river instead of trying to cross the stream just at the cabin's rear and so gain the cover of the trees more quickly, as he had originally proposed, and would have done but for the possibility that even on the opposite bank of the stream there were watchers in hiding.

But safe and certain as John's escape seemed to Ree, the truth was that during these past few minutes that young man had been in decidedly greater danger of losing his scalp than he cared ever to be again.

Creeping on hands and knees close to the wall whose dark background would help conceal his movements, John had made his way out of the barn and around to the rear of the cabin. Almost flat on his stomach, he drew himself slowly along the bluff and so descended to the valley where the river bank was not nearly so steep and comparatively low, rising only a few feet above the level of the water. Crawling cautiously along the narrow strip of slippery beach between the river's edge and the bank, he progressed steadily toward the woods. Often he paused to listen, and even when he moved on again he strained his ears and tried his utmost to see; but so deep was the darkness that, except for the denser black wall in the distance, which he felt rather than saw was the woods, he was certain that his situation, so far as seeing went, would be the same with his eyes shut as with them wide open.

In one of his pauses to hearken closer than he could do when moving, John thought he heard a low, hoarse "Ugh!" — an inarticulate sound, but one which seemed to express impatience, weariness, and "What's the use?" combined. He fancied he could see the shrug of the Indian's shoulders who, he was sure, was responsible for the guttural noise. For a long time the boy did not move. The rain came dripping down almost noiselessly. The wind whispered ever so softly in the lower parts of the valley and seemed to make no sound whatever save in the woods. To John it seemed that he waited an hour, though in fact it was but a few minutes. Over his shoulder he could see the ray of light from the cabin's open door. How far away it looked! Still that was fortunate. He would not have had it nearer for a great deal. Now he would try again. Softly — softly he raised one hand from the ground; softly, softly he raised a foot.

"Ugh!" Again it came; scarcely audible was the sound but the fierce howl of a wolf directly in his ears would not have startled, and frightened more the young white man crouching by the water.

The danger seemed nearer now — not more than three yards from him, John was certain — perhaps only two. He felt that he could put out his hand and touch the place from which it came. Again he was quiet, so quiet that he breathed in noiseless little gasps, a thing so trying on his throat and lungs that he would have felt as comfortable had he tried not to breathe at all.

But soon came another sound. Instantly John recognized it—the stealthy dipping of the paddle and low murmur of water against the nose of a canoe. Where was the canoe headed? That was the question. Toward him? Either that or up stream. The murmur of the current indicated that the craft ran not with it but against it. Now he heard the canoe touch the half submerged grass close in to shore. It was just abreast of him and within two arms' length. Now it grated ever so lightly upon the grass which, before the fall rains, had been quite up out of the water.

Again light as a feather came the dip of the paddle, again the soft murmur of the water barely heard above the quiet, even patter of the rain. At the same moment John felt himself slipping. Slowly the wet ground was giving way beneath him. He must move. It was a case of two dangers, either stand still and slide violently into the river, or move on a step and —

He must run the risk. Faster and faster he was sliding down. He must step quickly, and step quickly he did. He made no noise himself, he thought, but some pebble or bit of earth, loosened by his movement, rolled down and dropped with a splash into the water. Again came the muttered "Ugh!" something lower than before, and oh! Heaven be praised! no longer abreast but some yards from him.

Again came the low dipping of the paddle. They were patrolling the river for him, John knew now; but they would not find him. They might paddle silently up and down the whole night long, if they wished. In fact he rather hoped they would, and chuckled inwardly at the thought.

CHAPTER VI — "THE WITCH IS HIDDEN HERE."

That part of Lone-Elk's band which had been appointed to hide along the river bank throughout the day and paddle up and down in the densest shadows of the shores when night had come, did not keep up their search as long as John had hoped they would, when he silently chuckled over the thought of their waste of time and effort.

When they passed so close to the lad they sought, not more than one of them suspecting how very near he was, the Delawares were closing in on the cabin, together with others on shore. Lone-Elk had given the signal, by passing the word quietly along the irregular line his braves made around the clearing, after waiting all day long. He hoped to find the "witch" in hiding in the little cabin. Even if he did not, he would impress the Delawares with the seeming truth of the charge he had made against the young white man by showing that he was away from home, engaged, presumably, in some of his dreadful witch's work. The Seneca had, moreover, a plan in mind which made a visit to the home of the young Palefaces desirable from his point of view, whether the one they sought should be discovered or not, and now would be as good a time as any for the carrying out of his purpose.

While the Indians were yet at a distance, Kingdom, watching and listening in the cabin, heard their approach. He had kept his rifle close at hand all day, and now he casually picked the weapon up and with a show of idle carelessness polished its glossy stock with a bit of buckskin.

The savages came silently on, apparently without effort to keep from being heard. Kingdom was aware that they kept their line spread out so as to form a semicircle which, together with the river, would wholly enclose the little log house. His sharp ears assured him that this was done, but it was with well acted surprise that he sprang lightly up and stepped toward the door when Lone-Elk and one other Indian showed themselves at last within the dim ray of light shining from the fireplace.

"Come in! It's wet and bad outside! Bring them all in!" he called pleasantly, meeting the Seneca at the threshold and glancing out as if he plainly saw the whole line of Indians outside, which in fact he did not see at all.

"White Fox speaks kindly," answered Lone-Elk, calling Ree by the name the Delawares had long ago given him.

Only the Seneca and the one other Indian drew near the lighted space about the door, however, and these two now entered as if they were quite by themselves.

"Why should I not?" Ree answered to the Seneca's remark, noticing as he did so, how searchingly both the savages were looking about the cabin's single room. "We, — my white brother and myself — have had the friendship of the Delawares always."

"It is as the white brother says," said the second Indian, a powerful fellow whom Kingdom now recognized as a brave from the Delaware town on the Muskingum, and whom he had seen a number of times before. As he spoke, this Indian looked at Lone-Elk inquiringly. Perhaps the Seneca considered his words a challenge. At any rate he said sharply:

"Where is the other white brother! Does the White Fox wish to hide him then, if he is the friend of the Delawares? Will the White Fox hide the witch that breathed poison breath upon Big Buffalo, the witch that with a hatchet killed a Delaware warrior, yet left no mark?"

"What's this you say? What wild talk is this, Lone-Elk? Has Lone-Elk drunk of the firewater that he comes speaking so absurdly?"

Kingdom spoke with a show of temper and in a manner distinctly creditable to the part he was bound to act.

"It is the law that witches must be put to death," the Seneca returned vigorously. "Lone-Elk has said that Little Paleface with a witch's hatchet killed a Delaware warrior — killed Big Buffalo. Now must the witch be given up to the friends of him that was killed."

"Well, I can only tell you that the one you call Little Paleface is not here. He is far away and may not come back for some days," Kingdom answered quietly. "Now if Lone-Elk will believe this, and it is the truth, he will return to the town of the Delawares and I will myself go there tomorrow to have a talk. Is it a friendly thing for Delaware braves to remain hidden all about the lodge of their Paleface brothers as they are doing now? Let them all come into the light. Let them see that my brother who is accused so falsely — so unfairly and so unjustly — let them see, I say, that he is not here, and we will plan to have a talk tomorrow."

Lone-Elk gave a short, fierce whoop. Instantly fifteen or more Indians rushed into the cabin, crowding-the little room quite uncomfortably.

"The witch is hidden," said Lone-Elk, loudly. "If the Little Paleface is here let him show himself."

As Kingdom looked quickly from one to another of the Indians he observed with sorrow that Fishing Bird was among them. Had this good fellow turned against his white friends, too? But no, that quick friendly look as their eyes met was proof of his friendship still.

There being no answer to the Seneca's invitation to Little Paleface to show himself, except the grunted "Ughs!" of some of the Delawares, Lone-Elk sprang quickly up the ladder of poles and peered into the loft. Others followed his example, climbing up on stools or by the aid of the roughness of the wall. Some looked up the chimney. Some searched here, some there. One party of five or six, lighting hickory bark torches at the fire, went into the barn. In five minutes the whole cabin was turned topsy-turvy.

"You see it is just as I told you in the beginning," said Kingdom in a friendly tone, but somewhat impatiently. "Now will you not consent to a talk! Let it be in the Council House of the Delawares — let it be any place you choose. I think I can prove to you that this charge of witchcraft is placed against one who is as true and honest as ever man could be."

Ree was sorry to see that the Delawares looked to Lone-Elk to answer. He had more fear of this one Indian, under the circumstances, than of any other half dozen warriors in Captain Pipe's town.

"Let it be as the White Fox says," the Seneca answered. "Yet will my Paleface brother not deceive himself by thinking he deceives Lone-Elk. The Paleface witch but hides. If it is not so, let the witch come to the talk."

Not for a second did Kingdom allow this challenge to be unanswered. Like a flash every eye had turned to him; but instantly he said:

"Will the Seneca go to Fort Pitt and there put Little Paleface on trial before those whose customs are the customs of the Palefaces? No, of course he will not. And just so would it not be fair for Lone-Elk to demand more than he would be willing himself to give."

The justice of Kingdom's position was clear to the majority of the Indians and he could not help but notice it; still Lone-Elk's reply in curt, surly tones was far from pleasing.

"Yet the White Fox asks for a talk! Like squaws that tell one another of the worms that harmed the corn does the Paleface want the Delawares to meet together with him and speak idle words! Words! Words, that mean nothing and come to nothing."

With a move of his hand to his companions to follow, the Seneca left the cabin. Rapidly the other Indians marched off in single file after him. Fishing Bird, somehow, was the last to leave. As he went out of the door, he cast a glance of friendliness, which was also a look of warning, to Ree and the peace of mind of that young gentleman was not increased thereby.

By no means certain that the Indians would not return, Kingdom sat for a long time on the edge of his bunk, listening and thinking. He had great satisfaction in knowing that John was comparatively safe for the time, at least, and thankful, indeed, that his chum's departure had been so timely. He longed for another and more satisfactory talk with Fishing Bird. He must have such a talk, he resolved, if it could by any chance be arranged, before he undertook to show the Delawares that Big Buffalo had not been killed by witchcraft. Perhaps that friendly fellow would be able to give him the right clue to the whole situation. Might it not be he would frankly declare that it was by the hand of Lone-Elk, himself, that the warrior's life had been snuffed out!

In his own mind Ree had little doubt concerning the true cause of Big Buffalo's death; but by what means the Seneca had put out of his way the one member of Captain Pipe's community who openly resented his leadership there would most probably be a difficult question to answer.

So the lonely lad sat pondering a long time; how long he did not know or care. The rain was still falling, the wind still sighing dolefully when he arose at last, closed and barred the door, also barred the opening which served as a window, and removing only his moccasins lay down to rest. Repeatedly did he picture to his mind's eye John Jerome tramping slowly, silently through the wet leaves, among the dripping underbrush and trees, stopping often to get his bearings from the wind, and so making his weary and most lonesome way to the protection they had agreed upon.

Repeatedly his thoughts returned to the "big talk" which he must attend tomorrow; but sound sleep came to him at last, even while a crouching figure moved swiftly and stealthily into the clearing and paused as if in hiding behind a shock of corn—the very one on which the crow had perched in the afternoon—then stole on again and disappeared.

Even as the first object appeared, another approached the cabin and moved to the protection of the darker shadows of the stable. For a minute or two the figure stood quiet in the denser darkness beside the building, then moved cautiously toward the little cornfield as if attracted by a faint rustle of corn leaves which seemed to come from that vicinity.

The rain still fell in a quiet, unbroken drizzle, but the wind had abated and there was no reason to suppose that it caused the movement of the corn, which attracted the attention of the crouching creature. Still listening with utmost care, the crouching figure moved nearer to the spot from which the noise ensued.

To discern any object that was without motion, at a distance of even a few feet in the pitch darkness, was an impossibility; but as the rustling of the corn ceased, the one who had been attracted by the sound made out a stealthy movement in the vicinity and instantly stood still. When the darker shadow had passed beyond his vision he dropped to the ground and listened with his ear against the wet grass and earth. After a time he rose and ran forward ever so lightly, pausing at the edge of the woods.

Hour after hour passed. A dull gray light appeared on the clouds to the east. Rising then, and stretching himself, the silent watcher with frequent looks toward every point went directly to the barn built up against the white boys' cabin, opened the door and leaving it slightly ajar, sat down upon the floor in such a way that he could command a view of the greater part of the clearing.

The opening of the door of the barn made Return Kingdom move, sound asleep though he was, and directly he awoke, conscious of having heard some disturbing sound. What it was he did not know. For a time he listened, but finding that drowsiness was overcoming him, he roused himself with a sudden determination to investigate.

Springing up quietly, Kingdom put on his moccasins and opening a loophole, peeped out. Though still very dark inside the cabin, he could make out principal objects in the clearing, and noted nothing in the least unusual. Suppressing a most sleepy yawn, he decided to creep into his bunk and forget his troubles in restful unconsciousness until broad daylight came.

Very likely the noise which had wakened him was made by one of the horses, the lad thought. He peeped into the stable through a chink in the wall. Discovering immediately that the door of the lean-to was open, and remembering that he had closed it as usual, he was alarmed at once. He seized his rifle, unbarred the cabin door and rushed out.

As he swung wide the door of the stable, to learn the cause of it not being properly closed, a hand was held out to him and its mate was raised in a sign of silence.

Startled, Kingdom stepped back a pace, but before the other could speak he had recovered himself.

"Fishing Bird!" he exclaimed. "What in the world are you doing here at such a time as this, Fishing Bird?"

CHAPTER VII — THE SECRET LEAD MINE

"Listen, White Fox, listen, my Paleface brother," said Fishing Bird softly as he took Kingdom's hand and drew him gently into the barn; then dropping his voice to a whisper:

"Lone-Elk has been here. All night did Fishing Bird watch and follow him. Then Fishing Bird hid here for maybe Lone-Elk be coming back when white brother still was sleeping. Morning comes now. No more danger."

How to thank this friendly Indian Ree did not know. As he realized the hardship Fishing Bird had undergone to guard him from the wily, crafty Seneca, his voice trembled with emotion in trying to express his gratitude. Almost in the same breath he begged further information and an explanation of Lone-Elk's presence; asked to know how, in the darkness, the Delaware had been able to watch him without being himself discovered. Where had Lone-Elk gone? Why had he come at all?

Seated on a little mound of hay, well within the stable yet where he could readily see out, and dividing his attention between the clearing and Kingdom, who sat beside him, Fishing Bird told his story.

He had feared from the beginning that his warning to the two white boys to flee would be unheeded, he said, and so determined, since he could give them no assistance, that he would at least keep his eyes on Lone-Elk. The Delawares had accepted the proposal of the Seneca that the death of Big Buffalo be not allowed to break up the Harvest Festival entirely, and so the night of the feast day had been spent in merry-making, as the custom was.

With but little rest the morning after the festival, however, Fishing Bird went on in his own simple but honest way. Lone-Elk, calling on as many as wished to do so to accompany him, had set out for the house of the Palefaces. It was his purpose first to locate Little Paleface and catch him off his guard, lest by witchcraft he should bring harm to the Indians before they could lay hands on him, Fishing Bird explained. So all day the Indians had watched the cabin and kept themselves hidden so that they would not easily be seen even if in approaching their home the boys should come upon them suddenly from behind.

Lone-Elk told the Delawares that a crow, which flew down in the cornfield, was almost certainly Little Paleface himself, and as night came on he assured them that the witch would either be found in the cabin in the natural form of a man or be caught trying to escape in the form of a bird.

Some had asked why the witch would not simply become an animal or a cloud or some such thing and so easily evade them, but the Seneca's only answer to this was a growl at their ignorance and a hint that only children asked such questions.

Much that Fishing Bird told him was so nearly the same as Kingdom had previously guessed that the information was in no way surprising. But one thing which did surprise and interest him a great deal was the friendly Delaware's account of the escape of John Jerome.

Fishing Bird, having no belief in Lone-Elk's talk of witchcraft and being anxious to aid in the escape, rather than the capture of the so-called witch, was even more intent in watching all that went on than were any of the others, Lone-Elk excepted. In this way he accounted for his discovery of some object beside the river bank in the darkness as he and two other Delawares were paddling noiselessly toward the cabin — an object which he partially recognized, though none of the others so much as suspected its presence. Solely for the purpose of giving warning he had made sounds which would be heard and which, he was certain, had been heeded.

Ree could only thank his loyal friend again and again and he did not hesitate to tell the faithful fellow that he had almost certainly saved John Jerome from capture. This pleased Fishing Bird greatly. His pleasure was quite equal to that of a child which is praised for some duty well done.

"In fact," added Kingdom, putting his hand gratefully on the Delaware's arm, "we can never begin to pay you back for all you have done for us. But still you can help us so much more that I want to feel that I can depend on

47

you. I won't ask anything of you which is going to get you into trouble, and if I do, you must tell me. Neither do I want you to do anything or tell me anything which you do not feel that you can willingly do or tell. Is this fair and friendly, Fishing Bird?"

The Indian thoughtfully nodded.

"First then, why did Lone-Elk come back here in the night?"

The Delaware did not know and said so.

"I can guess that, anyhow," Kingdom went on. "But here's a more important question, Fishing Bird. Who, or what, do you think, killed Big Buffalo?"

The Indian shook his head. Kingdom scarcely knew whether he meant that he did not know or that he did not wish to tell. But he tried another question.

"Was it Lone-Elk?"

For a second or two there was no reply. "Yes, maybe Lone-Elk killed Big Buffalo," came the answer, but the tone even more than the words expressed doubt.

"Well, can you tell me this, Fishing Bird: What is the secret of the Seneca's power among the Delawares and why is he a wanderer and an outcast from his own nation and his own tribe? We all know that he is a sort of a fugitive, yet even Captain Pipe allows him the greatest liberty."

"Listen," said the Indian slowly and solemnly, "Paleface brothers must see always that no hurt comes to Lone-Elk, the Seneca. Yes, Lone-Elk is hated and Lone-Elk is hunted by his own people; but listen, White Fox, listen to this: Lone-Elk and no other knows where much lead for bullets is hidden in the ground. To Captain Pipe and to all the Delawares Lone-Elk brings lead—sometimes bullets, too—always lead. No, no! Lone-Elk will never show where lead comes from, so must no hurt come to him. Anything Paleface brother asks will Fishing Bird do, but if Lone-Elk dies who will know where lead is found! Lead placed in the ground by the Great Spirit for his children, the Delawares; for that is as Lone-Elk tells them."

Kingdom could not help smiling slightly at the simple earnestness of the Indian, but he was interested, too, greatly interested. Once or twice before he had heard Delawares make secret references to the finding of lead in the earth somewhere in the locality of the Cuyahoga river. Now he was convinced that a mine existed, the location of which was known only to the scheming Seneca.

"So that is why Captain Pipe harbors the fellow though he knows that his history is so bad," spoke Kingdom, partly to the Indian, partly to himself.

"White Fox knows how all the Indians look always now for much powder—much lead," the Delaware returned. He was thinking of the trouble along the border and the fighting which was sure to follow the march of "Mad Anthony" Wayne's army into the Indian country to avenge the killing of so many of St. Clair's men the year before.

Kingdom read Fishing Bird's meaning easily as print, though never until now had he realized how fully the redskins were planning for the expected battle, nor guessed how completely posted they were concerning the probable object of the troops Wayne was assembling on the Ohio below Fort Pitt.

"But you followed the Seneca, Fishing Bird. You watched him nearly all night, you say. Tell me, then, if Lone-Elk must not be harmed, what can you do, what am I to do if he makes trouble? Are we to let him drive Little Paleface from home—and me too? For of course if my friend cannot be with me, I shall not wish to stay here."

The friendly Delaware shrugged his shoulders and looked puzzled. Glancing up, however, and seeing that Kingdom was waiting for him to answer, he slowly shook his head. "Maybe White Fox can find how Big Buffalo died. Maybe Palefaces can tell Captain Pipe that and then Lone-Elk can talk of witches no more."

"Yes, but what if Lone-Elk kills somebody before somebody can do this?" Ree inquired.

"When Lone-Elk comes to do that then Lone-Elk must be killed," Fishing Bird admitted rather reluctantly. But to show that he meant what he said, he now told at some length how he had followed the Seneca from the Delaware village all the way back to the cabin of the two white boys, when he found the crafty fellow stealing away after the return from the fruitless watch and search for John Jerome the preceding day and night. He left no room for doubt that he would have given Kingdom warning of the fellow's presence if necessary; but Ree could not help but believe that his friend had also some other reason for spying upon Lone-Elk's movements.

"This 'talk' I am to have with your people today,—will it do any good, Fishing Bird?" Kingdom at last inquired.

"All the Delawares ask how came Big Buffalo to die," was the Indian's only answer; and presently, though Kingdom asked him to remain, he slipped away, and wading the river at a place not usually used for crossing, quickly disappeared in the thick brush of the western bank.

In spite of the restless night he had spent and his weariness and anxiety, Ree made all possible haste with his breakfast and morning work in house and barn and hastened away to meet John Jerome. He must carry some provisions to him and let him know all that he had heard before starting for the Delaware town.

The distance to the place of meeting which the two boys had finally agreed upon was four miles or more, the spot a well hidden gully running back from the river until it lost itself in a dense growth of underbrush. From the midst of this matted mass there sprang up a great hollow whitewood tree with a large opening at the base. The lads had once hidden some traps there and knew the place well. In this natural shelter they would be quite free from possible observation, and anything left there would be little likely to be found by straggling Indians hunting in the vicinity.

With much anxiety Kingdom approached the meeting place. The day had come on dull and cloudy but still and in the vast silence of the leaf-carpeted forest the moist air made his every footfall seemingly loud and heavy. Yet listen as he did, even holding his breath, Ree heard not a sound to indicate that he would find John waiting for him. This was the more surprising because of Jerome's customary carelessness so far as being very quiet was concerned.

Even when he reached the thicket in which the old whitewood stood, Kingdom listened in vain for the slightest signal to indicate that his coming was expected. He had had no doubt John would be at the place long before he himself arrived. What else would he have to do save wait and watch?

"Covered his trail better than he usually does if he has been anywhere near here!" Ree ejaculated beneath his breath when, after making the entire circuit of the mass of underbrush, he found nothing. Heavy hearted, he sat down with his back to a large maple to wait.

Now what Kingdom should have done, of course, was to make his investigation thorough before he concluded that John had not come. Ordinarily he would have done so — would have gone to the bottom of the subject before he reached a final conclusion; but as many another has done before and since he let a peck of troubles become greater still by shouldering some with which he might much better not have burdened himself, taking for granted, as it were, that trouble was his portion.

It was and is a bad thing to do. The fact was that while Kingdom waited on and on, trying not to worry, but thinking very unhappy thoughts indeed, John Jerome, curled among some dry leaves in the base of the great hollow tree, snoozed as composedly as ever he did in his far away home in Connecticut.

Kingdom rose to his feet. Something must be done! He shook off his heavy thoughts and stood for a moment to consider. It was the movement of his rising, perhaps, that awakened John. He, also, rose to his feet. He heard soft footsteps among the leaves and peeped out. He heard them more plainly and hurried cautiously to a part of the thicket from which he could see beyond the brush. There was Kingdom marching away through the woods as if he were going somewhere and in a hurry to arrive.

A whistle which might have been the call of a squirrel sounded. It was a signal both boys used for each other in the woods, and in another instant the needless burden had rolled off Ree's mind. What a sea of fresh difficulties must certainly have come to both of them but for the chance awakening of John, in the nick of time, the two boys did not long discuss.

"But you would have come into the tree to leave some grub for me, anyway, Ree," said John.

"Hanged if I thought of such a thing!" Kingdom answered. "You don't deserve it, nohow! Going to sleep and keeping me in such a stew about you!" he added good-naturedly.

The lads were both seated on the ground inside the protecting whitewood now, and John, having long since eaten the provisions with which he left home, was making good use of those Ree brought. He had, he declared, with venison in one hand and bread in the other, a more immoderate appetite than any well-behaved witch should ever have.

John's friendly feeling for Fishing Bird was certainly not diminished by what Ree told him concerning the good turns the faithful Delaware had done both of them. He quickly verified the statement that he had been warned by the voice of Fishing Bird at the brink of the river the night before, though he had little suspected the source from which came the "Ughs" he heard.

More than all else, however, excepting Ree's own personal safety at the cabin, was John interested in the hidden lead mine of which Lone-Elk alone possessed definite knowledge. He declared at once his intention of improving his time in exile by watching the woods for the Seneca and following him wherever he went.

"You'll do nothing of the kind, my boy," said Kingdom with playful affection, but yet very earnestly. "I more than half suspect that one reason Fishing Bird follows and watches Lone-Elk is the expectation that he will find out where the mine is. With two of you on the Seneca's trail, it is altogether too certain that he will find you out. And, mark this good and seriously, John, there's no doubt whatever but that Lone-Elk would rather scalp you than not. I don't think for a minute, mind you, that he believes his own witch stories. But he means business in the whole bad mess he has made for us. I'm confident he will not bother me very much, but for all practical purposes he has full permission and authority to take your topknot the first chance he gets. It's the witch law of pretty much all the Indians and of all the Iroquois. The Delawares have all the Iroquois customs from having been subject to them for so long, years ago. So we know what we will have to reckon with."

Jerome was rather inclined to demur but Kingdom would not hear to arty plan but that he should remain carefully in hiding.

"Well, then, I'll tell you what I'll do," John suggested, as a final effort to gain more freedom than Ree believed wise, "I'll take two or three days to myself and make a pilgrimage to the 'salt lick' over by the Mahoning river. Oh, I'll be wary! I'll look sharp enough, don't you fear!" he added, seeing what Ree was about to say.

And so it was agreed that while Kingdom undertook to clear up the mystery of the death of Big Buffalo, Jerome should keep himself occupied and out of sight by the journey he proposed. The plan, like many another plan, far more carefully deliberated upon, had, as events proved, a most important bearing on the future.

But no man can tell what the next day, aye, the next hour, the next minute, will bring forth, however much our every act is constantly shaping the unknown fate and future.

CHAPTER VIII – THE SALT SPRINGS – A STARTLING DISCOVERY

Besides the much traveled path extending south from the river on which the cabin of the youthful pioneers was situated, to the main branch of the Muskingum, there was another thoroughfare of the Indians in the vicinity. The general direction of its course was east and west. This trail was not used a great deal, but it was, for the most part, along its route that the two boys had first made their way into the Ohio wilds two years before. At occasional intervals Delawares and others followed this path in traveling toward Fort Pitt, or in journeying from that point to Sandusky and the country of the Wyandots near the lake, farther to the west or to the Maumee which lay beyond.

At a distance of two days' journey eastward from the cabin on the Cuyahoga, a branch of this trail forked off and led on to a much frequented "salt lick" or spring of salty water, near the Mahoning river. To this "lick" the Indians came from far and near to make salt. Settlers came from great distances, also, especially in later years, to boil the waters of the springs, and Kingdom and Jerome had known of the place for a long time.

Having first heard of the "big lick" from the Delawares, the boys had verified the information so obtained by talking with hunters and traders. Often had they planned to visit the place. During the winter, when work in their clearing was less pressing, they frequently had said they would obtain a year's supply of salt for themselves. But that was before trouble had come to them. What they would do now must depend entirely upon future developments.

Kingdom saw no good reason for John's proposed trip to the "lick," but neither did he see a reason for not going; besides, maybe it would be better for Jerome to be away from the locality in which such grave danger threatened him, and the more especially so in view of the temptation he would have to try to find the secret lead mine of the outcast Seneca.

Thus the two friends parted. Kingdom had already lost much time. He feared being late at the council he was to have with Captain Pipe's principal people and much as he would have liked to go a little way with John, he felt that he must hurry directly to the cabin.

No sooner was Ree gone from the hollow whitewood, however, than John Jerome found interest in the trip to the "lick" suddenly lagging. It was one thing to talk to his bosom friend about the undertaking, but quite another to sit solitary and alone pondering upon its hardships. But he was in for it now. It most certainly would not do to give up. Kingdom would not expect to see him for four or five days at least, and he would be alone for that length of time anyway, he reflected. Thus in a measure he restored his first enthusiasm for the journey he had so impulsively suggested, and ten minutes later was on the way.

To have followed the old trail which led toward the salt spring would have been, from John's starting point, considerably out of his way. It lay much to the south. To travel through the unbroken woods would be harder but it would likewise be safer and the latter was an important point to consider. So through the woods, setting himself to make nearly a bee line to the east, the lonesome young woodsman tramped. Sleep and food had much refreshed him after the labor and the adventures of the night, however, and except for the sense of loneliness and something of worry and anxiety concerning Kingdom's safety, which hung heavily upon his thoughts, he would have been in fine spirits.

John was quite familiar with that portion of the woods which he was now traversing. It was not far from here that he had been held captive in the cave where dwelt Duff and Dexter. Over to the right a mile or so was the spot where the unscrupulous Duff, himself, had been forced to surrender and beg for his very life. On ahead was the little lake where Captain Brady had hidden, a number of years before. John and Ree had hunted up the place one time, just to see the spot after hearing of Brady's wonderful leap and exciting adventure from some settlers near Fort Pitt.

The leaves underfoot and all the great forest stretching away for miles on every side were still wet from the drenching rain of the previous night.

Any trail made the day before must needs have been well marked or all traces of it would be now obliterated. John thought of this as in the course of the day's travel he twice came upon signs which seemed to tell of some person or persons having passed through much the same portion of the wilds as he was traveling, within a few days at most. One sign of this kind was a freshly cut mark of a hatchet upon a great, smooth-barked beech. Another was the presence of one small stone beside a large one and a small quantity of hickory nut shells.

No thought of danger because of these indications that there were other travelers in the woods came to Jerome. The mark upon the beech tree might have been made by anyone, white man or red. It merely showed that some one had recently been there. Likewise the nut shells may have been left by a chance hunter or even by a party of them. Still, having found these signs, and feeling quite interested in discovering more of them, some which might reveal more definite facts perhaps, as the ashes of a campfire, for example, John looked keenly in all directions as he tramped on and on. But he saw nothing and the necessity of searching for something he deemed more important—a safe and comfortable place to spend the night—caused him to turn his thoughts to other things as the short fall day drew early to a close.

A tangled mass of wild grapevines hanging over a little gully, and sheltering it alike from wind and rain, seemed to offer a good prospect, but turned out a disappointment. The ground, on being inspected, proved exceedingly wet. So on John went. Once he paused beside the thickly spreading branches of a maple, which had been uprooted by some summer storm, and contemplated lying down among the leaves the breezes had collected there. But he shook his head and passed by.

"Why the very mischief I ever thought of coming on this wild goose chase I don't know, I vow!" the young wayfarer grumbled to himself, with a grim frown.

He was thinking of the snug little log house and the warm supper and warm bed he might have had in prospect. Even the shelter of the projecting ledge of rock, whose protection he had had the night before, seemed very attractive now. "And the old hollow poplar, that would be quite a lord mayor's mansion, for a fact it would!" he told himself. "But there's no use fussing for what you haven't got and can't have," he added, with a philosophy which many an older man has never learned, and walked on the faster.

Only once or twice before had John spent a night in the open woods without Kingdom for company, and though he was not afraid, he dreaded the hours of darkness and the lonesome, cheerless night now just before him more and more as the shadows thickened.

"Howl away, you pesky rascals! Howl away! But you don't know what you're howling for!" he burst out almost spitefully as the yelping of wolves reached his ears. "I'm not going to climb a tree on your account—not if I don't have to," he added, making the latter saving clause barely audible, even to himself.

A strange place for a night's rest it was which John selected at last as a final choice. "But," as he reasoned with his protesting, tired-out body, "you've got to take what you can get and take it mighty quick at that, if you are going to see what you're getting."

The resting place thus selected was a chestnut tree which sent out four branches a few feet above the ground, each as large as an ordinary tree, and each spreading broadly in a different direction from the others. The effect was to form at the place from which the branches projected a seat by no means uncomfortable and having the advantage of being high and dry, at least. Indeed, John found that by sitting astride of one great limb and leaning against another, he not only maintained his balance easily but rested comparatively well. With his blanket wrapped round him and over his head like a hood, he ate his supper of dried venison, wished he had a drink, decided it was too much trouble to go for one, fell to thinking of the absurdity of Lone-Elk's accusations and drifted off to sleep.

Before morning John felt severely the effects of being so long in one position, but nothing worse disturbed him. He heard wild creatures of the forest all about at different times in the night, but even had human eyes come very close they would hardly have seen in the thick darkness the solitary figure perched in the chestnut's forks. But it was a genuine luxury to be on the ground and feel the cushions of leaves-underfoot once more; and so it was, while he strode steadily forward, facing always the east, that John ate his meager breakfast.

Watchful as he always was to obtain fresh clues to the presence of others than himself in any portion of the woods, John still found nothing to interest him particularly. In the afternoon he came upon a runway of the deer, and confident from its general trend that it led toward the salt springs, he followed it. He came upon various indications that the path had been used by two-footed as well as four-footed creatures. Once he found the skeleton of a large buck. Near by was a sapling which had been bent down over the path, and a long withe made into a noose close at hand, showed how the poor creature died.

None of the things he saw, however, conveyed to John any thought but that he must be nearing the salt "lick" now; and that perhaps he would find some one there, and would do well to be very careful as he approached, not knowing whom he might find, and being somewhat particular who might find him.

Even when he picked up a buckskin glove with spatters of blood upon it beside the runway, John had no presentiment of what was to come. He only muttered: "White folks at the spring now, or have been there not long ago, at least. Settlers, probably. You don't catch anybody else putting on mittens before it has even snowed. What a big hand he had!"

The concluding exclamation followed the trying on of the glove. It was, indeed, a large one, and because of its size and not knowing just where to carry it, John was inclined to throw it down by the path and leave it; but he reconsidered and tucked the buckskin in his belt. He found it there, convenient for reference, when a decidedly startling discovery somewhat later brought the glove very forcibly to his recollection.

The runway of the deer brought the boy at last to a considerable stream which he rightly guessed to be the river, known to the Indians then and to everyone now as the Mahoning. The path skirted its banks for some distance, then turned into the woods again, leading on to the springs of slightly salty water which lay at no great distance.

Only by hard traveling had John reached the place before nightfall, but he was thankful for his rare good fortune in doing so. To spend several hours at least in locating the "lick," after he had come fairly into its vicinity, was what he had expected, and now to come directly to the spot was indeed lucky. He had never seen the place before but he could not doubt the evidence that lay on every hand. Indeed, he was greatly surprised to find so many indications that the springs were often visited.

They lay in an open space of two or three acres, grown up to low bushes and rank grass, save for the paths where the ground had been tramped bare by the deer and other animals. In several places were the ashes of long-deserted campfires. Near the border of the clearing were two or three rough, quickly-erected log cabins. But these also, were deserted, and toppling over from neglect. The spring or springs — for the water seemed to bubble forth in two or three places — were enclosed by heavy planks, hewed from whole trees, forming a vat nearly six paces square, as John measured it, and rather more than three feet deep. This vat was sunk in the ground and as the astonished young visitor lay down to drink from it, what was his surprise to discover two large iron kettles at its bottom, plainly visible in the clear, sparkling water.

With rare interest the young explorer looked upon his discoveries. Another thing which much attracted him were pits that had been dug as hiding places by hunters, wherein they lay in wait for the coming of deer to the springs at night. These may have been the work of white men or of Indians, for it was not many miles, John knew, to the old Indian village which he had heard called Mahoning Town. He doubted if many Indians lived there, now, however,—not more than one or two families at most he thought—for at this distance from the border, the homes of the Mingoes, which once had been occupied, were already falling to ruins. The inhabitants of the villages had moved farther into the wilderness or were scattered and there seldom remained so much as a dog to bark at strangers.

John was somewhat disappointed to find no white person or persons near, and no sign that any had been there since the rain of the second night before, at least. But it was lucky, on the other hand, that he found no hostile Indians there, and just at that time it would have been pretty hard to tell which redskins were hostile and which were not, unless one personally knew them.

So, having satisfied himself that neither friend nor foe was in the vicinity, the interested young discoverer again drank heartily of the spring's very pleasant waters and then calmly sat down at some little distance to rest and survey the situation more leisurely than he had done at first.

The salt "lick" or spring was somewhat to one side of a wide, shallow valley. The extent to which the vicinity had been frequented had caused many trees and much brush to be cleared away, as in the course of time they had been burned and chopped down to provide wood for the making of salt or the building of huts. The effect was to make the woods quite open all about the little clearing. But, notwithstanding, it was a very desolate, lonely spot. The wind blew in a most melancholy manner and the impression came to John that the springs were haunted. Surely if ghosts ever appeared anywhere in the whole vast wilderness, here was a place which seemed the very one at which they would assemble. But it was for the sake of security from being found by living visitors to the "lick" that the lad decided he would do well to go farther into the forest to spend the night. This he did, and as it was now dusk, he sought a safe resting place with great eagerness.

Knowing that creatures of all sorts would be likely to come to the spring after darkness set in — even buffalos, though they were exceedingly rare in these parts, John was well aware — the lad had no excuse to make to his courage in looking for a tree which would offer a comfortable perch. This he failed to find, but high up on the hillside to the east of the "lick" he found, as he searched further, a rude shack or shelter built up with poles and brush, probably by salt boilers. At least there was a considerable bed of ashes in front of the open side of the brush wind-shield, and under cover and comparatively dry was a bed of small boughs, leaves and long, wild grass, such as grew in the valley below.

The effect of this discovery upon John Jerome was to make him feel quite at home. The dreary prospect of spending an uncomfortable night vanished. If others had found it safe to have a campfire and sleep like civilized mortals, why should not he? A campfire and all the comforts of the brush house should be his, he instantly decided, let the consequences be what they might. So the next half hour was busily spent in gathering firewood.

With dry leaves and powder and the exercise of patience, born of the days which knew not matches, John kindled his fire. He chose not to risk more than a small blaze, however, and by starting it very close to the front of the shack made its ruddy glow scarcely visible from one direction, at least. The principal advantage of this was in having the fire close to him as he lay on the bed of tender boughs; still he was glad to think that he was "being prudent," as Return Kingdom would wish him to be, though he smiled at the thought.

Good, honest fatigue and a clear conscience put John to sleep early, despite the troubled state of his mind whenever he thought of his enforced absence from the only home he had. If prowlers of any kind, man or beast, were near him while darkness lasted, he did not know it. He awoke to find the dawn breaking and, knowing that he must soon start back to keep his appointment with Ree, set out at once for another inspection of the salt spring and its surroundings.

How he chanced to come upon it or what prompted him to pause before it, there is no necessity of telling, but certain it is that when about to leave the spring, John found at a distance of forty rods to the west of the "lick," on a slight rise of ground, a pile of brush in the midst of a sumac thicket.

"How did it get there and what's the purpose of it?" he asked himself, wondering if it were not a trap for wild turkeys.

With a determination to find an answer to his questions, he pushed in among the bushes and pulled the low brush pile to one side.

A ghastly sight confronted him. Dead, their skins discolored, their clothing hanging loosely on their gaunt bodies, stiff and cold, their scalps gone, were two men—two young men—who, it was evident, had come from the settlements.

CHAPTER IX—THE EVIL POWER OF LONE-ELK

Perspiring and thirsty after his long, rapid walk from the hollow poplar to the cabin, Kingdom would gladly have rested before going on to the town of the Delawares, but the day was already well advanced and he must hurry. Stopping only for a drink of water, therefore, and to assure himself that nothing had been disturbed in his absence, he saddled Phoebe and was away again.

The boy had been thinking much of all that he meant to say to Captain Pipe and his counselors and the subject still occupied him as he drew near the Indian village. He glanced anxiously about, wondering if he would be met by any such warning as had come to him the day before, but saw no one. Going on to the straggling little collection of huts of bark and skins which comprised the town, however, he was soon greeted by Captain Pipe himself and a score of warriors. The manner of the Indians was very formal and cool, yet not especially unfriendly, Kingdom thought, and he felt sure that if it were not for Lone-Elk he could win all the friends of the dead Big Buffalo over to his side and persuade them that witchcraft had not been the cause of death.

Lone-Elk was not present when Kingdom arrived, but scarcely had the lad tied his horse when the Seneca came stalking forth from his lodge, a wigwam made of skins, and followed the chief and the other Indians as they led the way with Ree to the Council House. The latter building was the same as that in which the religious exercises of the Harvest Festival were held and has been sufficiently described.

Captain Pipe and his followers ranged themselves in a wide semicircle at one side of the long, low structure and Kingdom sat opposite them. Lone-Elk was at the extreme left of the line of warriors on the chief's right. He had not spoken to the white visitor, nor did he now deign to take any notice of him. In all respects his conduct and general bearing were not only insolent but ugly to the point of savage hostility.

When all were seated, Captain Pipe briefly said that the council was ready to hear any message or statement which the Paleface visitor wished to present.

Kingdom had hoped he would have an opportunity to learn something more than he yet knew as to the circumstances of Big Buffalo's death before the council convened, but there had been no time for this, and he could but make the best of his situation.

Rising, Ree saluted the Indians very respectfully and began what proved to be a really able speech, though he had little supposed that so much formality would be observed in the "talk" he had asked to have. From quiet, slowly spoken words, Kingdom advanced by degrees to louder tones and greater vehemence, and he had, he was glad to see, the respectful attention of every Indian present, not excepting Lone-Elk.

On the latter's face an expression of indifferent insolence changed to one of very attentive thoughtfulness. He realized that here was a force and an appeal to the reason and intelligence of the Delawares which might very easily prove the undoing of his schemes and his accusations and possibly end most unfortunately for himself.

Kingdom spoke most plainly, and understanding full well the power of hard, honest truth, honestly and forcefully presented, he frankly owned that John Jerome had been forced into hiding by the danger in which he was placed, owing to the charge that was made against him. They both would be compelled to leave their home and lose it and all the work they had done in their clearing if the Delawares could not be made to see that this accusation of witchcraft was unjust and false, he said. He reminded Captain Pipe and the others how, in good faith, he and John had bought their land; how they had refrained from going to the west of the river on the portage path because those lines marked the boundary of the lands the Indians had never surrendered to the white people as a whole. He appealed to the sense of justice which every Indian had, to the end that they might see how unfair it was to take the testimony of any one person as conclusive evidence of guilt.

Neither did Ree spare the Seneca. He warmly called attention to the character of Lone-Elk and denounced the fellow as an outcast, a fugitive from the villages and the haunts of his own people; scored him as one whose history made him an unfit witness for the Delawares to believe, and especially so since the accusation he made was directed against one whose friendship for all the Delawares, Big Buffalo included, had been proved time and again.

Much more did Ree say, and he was satisfied as he finished that, whatever the outcome might be, he had done his best. He had suggested many causes for Big Buffalo's sudden death, any one of which he declared was more reasonable than this idea of witchcraft. He had asked that the opportunity be given him to examine the body of the dead warrior to see if he could not then tell precisely what had produced death. He would not say, he stated, that he could positively do this, but it would be no more than fair to let him try.

In accordance with the Indian custom, when matters of such grave concern were the subject of a council, Kingdom withdrew after he had presented his contention to await a decision when the Delawares had discussed the matter among themselves.

What went on in the Council House while he walked about outside Kingdom did not know. He easily imagined that Lone-Elk would ridicule things that he had said and ask if he himself had not been as good a Delaware since coming among them as any warrior present.

Ree's guess was not far wrong. Lone-Elk did appeal to Captain Pipe and everyone present in the strongest language at his command, reiterating again and again that what his eyes bad seen should stand for more than any denial which the young Palefaces could make. And he promised, too, that if the opportunity were given him, he would find evidence convincing to every Delaware that the Little Paleface was a witch and that he and no other had caused the death of the warrior whose arm would be lifted in battle, whose voice would sound upon the warpath never again.

For more than an hour the council remained in session while Kingdom walked up and down impatiently among the low huts. Most of the Indians of both sexes were gathered in the Council House and he was quite alone. A step near by stirred him from his melancholy revery. Glancing up, he found Fishing Bird beside him. The look on the friendly fellow's face was enough to tell Ree that the council had decided against him.

"Come," the Indian said, telling with his eyes that which he dared not speak, and Kingdom followed him into the long, bark building and once more stood before the council.

Very gravely Captain Pipe motioned to the white boy to be seated, and himself rising, spoke slowly and with much earnestness in English, which language he now used quite fluently.

At considerable length the Delaware chief reviewed the whole case which had been presented both by Ree and by Lone-Elk, the accuser. He criticised the "Paleface brother" for having failed to bring before the council the one who had been accused. He praised Ree, however, for the frank and open way in which he had laid his arguments before the Indians and for the friendliness he had shown the Delawares at all times.

About the boundary between the white nation and the Indian nations, Captain Pipe said it was true that a treaty had been made several years earlier by the white people and the Delaware, Chippewa and Wyandot nations (at Fort Industry, in 1785) in which it was agreed that the Indians would give up all claim to the land east of the Cuyahoga river, the portage path and the Tuscarawas river, or main branch of the Muskingum, as it was also called. He said further that this same treaty was renewed at a somewhat later time (at Fort Harmer, in 1789) when the Delawares, Wyandots, Chippewas, Sacs and Pottawatomies had made an agreement with the Palefaces.

That the treaties were not kept, Captain Pipe declared, was the fault of the white people because they were always encroaching upon the lands of the Indians and always seeking to drive them farther and farther to the west. He could not consider, he said, that the two young white settlers had any rights in the Ohio country except that which came to them by reason of their having traded goods for the certain small parcel of land they occupied. If they wished to hunt or fish on any other land excepting the few acres they owned, they did so only because the Indians permitted it. Therefore if any violation of Indian laws or customs was committed, they must answer to the Indians for the violation and not contend, as White Fox had done, that a trial by the people of their own color and laws was their right, because they did not actually live on Indian soil.

The agreement the council had reached in regard to the charge of witchcraft against him who was called "Little Paleface," Captain Pipe at last concluded, was that Lone-Elk and others should go forth to search for further evidence against the white boy. Further, it was agreed that the Delawares would grant the White Fox — meaning Ree — permission to try to show that Big Buffalo died from some cause other than witchcraft if he would give himself as a hostage for the delivery of Little Paleface into the hands of Lone-Elk, in case it was finally decided that witchcraft actually caused the death of the warrior whose voice was now silent.

The latter proposition came as a decided surprise to Kingdom. He had been prepared to hear the decision that Lone-Elk have the opportunity to produce evidence. He remembered vividly now the secret visit the Seneca had paid the clearing the night before. But he dared not speak of it. To do so would betray Fishing Bird. And not knowing what Lone-Elk would "find" in the way of "evidence," Ree was much at a loss to answer when Captain Pipe, bidding him speak, sat down.

Like the ingenious Yankee boy that he was, Ree did not reply at once to the hostage part of the Delaware chief's proposal. Concerning the search for evidence, he could only say, he stated, that full permission was given the

Indians to look in every nook and corner of the cabin by the river and in the clearing and the woods surrounding it, or wherever else they chose. If they found anything which could be taken to be evidence that John Jerome had aught to do with the death of Big Buffalo, it would be something which had been placed among their property by others; it would be "made to order" evidence, and therefore worth nothing to any fair minded member of the Delaware or any other nation.

Having spoken thus far, and thinking now of the offer that he give himself as a hostage, though he did not mention it, Ree asked of Captain Pipe and all the Indians present whether he was to consider them personally as friends or foes. He wanted to know whether he himself was to be free to come and go as in the past, or whether it was their intention to dispossess him of his land by practically driving him off of it.

"If you do this," said he, "in what way is it better than the treatment the Indians themselves complain of, that they are driven from their forests?"

The thought thus presented interested Captain Pipe a great deal and for a second or two he did not answer.

"The council is over. The Paleface brother knows its decision. It is not the custom to talk when the time for talking is past," he said at last.

"Yes, but am I to be molested? Am I to lie down at night knowing that to me, personally, at least, the Delawares are friends, or am I to watch lest as enemies they come to kill me?" Ree demanded.

"The Paleface brother gives himself not as a hostage. He has rejected the offer made him," Captain Pipe answered.

"I want only time to think about that," said Ree. "I will answer later."

The council was over but the Indians all remained silent, listening attentively to everything which was said. Inquiringly now they looked to their chief to know the white boy's fate. Most of them felt friendly toward him. But at the same time all, or nearly all, were growing daily more hostile to the whites in general.

"The White Fox may go. He is free and no Indian will disturb him; but he must come no more to the village of the Delawares if he comes not as a hostage. He must remain near his own lodge and if he goes from his own land he must go not far. He must carry no tales of what the Indians are doing to the forts or to the houses of the Paleface people. On the land that the Delawares sold to him the Paleface brother shall be as safe as the eagle in its nest upon the mountain tops."

"No other place, though," Lone-Elk grunted savagely and only half audibly.

Whether Captain Pipe heard him Ree did not know, for as the latter had ceased speaking he had dismissed the council with a wave of his hand, and now all the Indians were moving toward the open air, some quiet and thoughtful, some talking, some pushing and hurrying, some inclined to linger.

Gentle Maiden was among the latter. She passed very near Ree as she moved slowly out and, unobserved by any save himself, gave the lad a glance which was most friendly, the only really friendly look he had received except from Fishing Bird.

With an effort Kingdom suppressed a tear of bitterness and disappointment which, somehow, the friendly look from the Indian girl had brought to his eyes. He waited only until he could reach Captain Pipe and shake his hand to show the appreciation and respect which he felt were really due the chief, sadly misled by Lone-Elk though the proud Delaware was. Ree could not but notice Hopocon performed the friendly ceremony of shaking hands with far less of cordial warmth than usual.

"So much," he thought, "for the fact that Captain Pipe needs lead and that the Seneca knows where lead is."

But he said good-bye to those who were near, untied Phoebe and rode slowly away. The day was very near its close.

CHAPTER X—"MORE BULLETS, MORE LEAD."

Ree did not doubt that Lone-Elk, expecting that he and John would meet to talk over the events of the day and the outcome of the "talk," would either spy upon him as he made his way home, or keep watch of the clearing during the night.

The lad easily saw in the Seneca the influence which set Captain Pipe and many of the other Delawares against him and against John. He concluded, too, that so far as Lone-Elk was concerned, the accusation of witchcraft was but a means to an end.

He was certain that the Seneca had some evil purpose in view in causing the Delawares to believe the absurd things he told them. Or was it only to shield himself from suspicion in connection with Big Buffalo's death that he had invented the witchcraft story? Was the Seneca, then, really the murderer of the Delaware warrior? If he were not, he must have some reason for turning the people of Captain Pipe's village against their white neighbors other than merely to avert suspicion from himself.

Often the worn and anxious boy recalled the warning Captain Pipe had given him to carry to the settlements no news of what the Indians were doing. Could it be that some attack upon Gen. Wayne's men was being planned and the Delawares, inspired by Lone-Elk, were afraid the white boys would hear of it and give the alarm? Or did Lone-Elk merely fear the Paleface pioneers would discover the secret lead mine which gave him his hold upon Captain Pipe? Maybe that keen old redskin himself feared the same thing and dreaded lest the white soldiers should invade the country to win possession of so rich a prize.

Ree wondered if he was right in any of these surmises, then it would seem that the wish of the Indians was to cause him and John to forsake their cabin and their clearing and be gone to return no more. On the other hand, after the warning he had received, it would be positively unsafe for him to travel far in the direction of Fort Pitt or the settlements, lest the redskins suspect him of going to betray some secret, and so make an end of him. What then could he do?

So, completely tired out after the past two anxious days and nights, Kingdom floundered more and more hopelessly in a sea of "ifs" and "but thens," and confused question marks, as he tried in vain to arrive at what would seem to him a correct summing up of the situation.

"It's just no use thinking any more about it," he declared to himself when half way home. But he added, "Not now, at least," as a second thought, for he well knew in what direction his mind would turn when he had rested and could reflect with more composure.

A half mile from the Delaware town Ree had let Phoebe gallop wherever the trail was open enough to make such speed possible, and he had a grim satisfaction in the belief that Lone-Elk was following him.

The Seneca was equal to such a task. Nothing tired him; no hardships or labor were tod great for him to undertake when he had a point to gain. Kingdom knew this well. He saw in the hateful fellow a spirit which nothing could turn aside and a strength and cunning far superior to the same qualities in other Indians, though all were gifted in this way.

"I only hope he is following. If I could be sure of it and make him run his legs half off to keep up, only to disappoint him in the end, I'd gallop you every step, Phoebe, every last step," Ree told the sagacious mare, who was picking her steps with the utmost nicety.

And the fact was that the tenacious Seneca, thinking that Kingdom would surely go at once to his companion, was following the horse and rider at no great distance behind. He was afraid to go forward to the clearing, and spy upon the cabin from the edge of the woods lest Ree meet John at some appointed place along the trail. He thought with savage pleasure of the satisfaction he would have in dragging the Little Paleface before the assembled Delawares. With a sort of fierce happiness he anticipated the pride and joy he would have in hanging the white boy's scalp above the door of his lodge where all might see.

Forced as he was to run at a good, round speed in order to keep the sound of the horse's hoofs within hearing, and being tired and in no pleasant frame of mind to begin with, Lone-Elk became furious as mile after mile he followed on and all to no purpose. His very scowl was frightful. Again and again was he tempted to overtake the young white man and vent his hatred in one safe, sure shot from behind.

Had the Seneca attempted to put this thought into execution, however, he would certainly have regretted it. Unknown to him, Fishing Bird was also on the trail. Keenly as Lone-Elk followed the horse and rider, he in turn was spied upon by the Delaware who, for a favor done him long ago, was willing to risk his life for his Paleface friend.

As Kingdom reached the clearing and mounted the hill to the log house, Lone-Elk changed his course and traversed the edge of the woods to a point from which he could command a view of the cabin and the whole open space about it. Fishing Bird changed his course also. From behind a clump of hazel bushes he kept his eyes on the Seneca unceasingly.

Long after the firelight shone brightly from the door of the white boys' home, Lone-Elk, silent as the very tree trunk which screened him, watched and waited. Scarcely could Fishing Bird see him, yet with equal patience, he also remained at his post.

Little guessing how closely his every movement was scrutinized by eyes in which there was not one gleam of kindness or of justice, Kingdom went about his evening work in the barn and house and prepared his lonely supper. One consoling thought, and only one, came to him. It was that he could consider himself safe for the present. He would have time to meet John when he returned, and then if they agreed that their only safety lay in deserting the cabin,—the cabin and all they had accomplished in the clearing,—they would do so. With a few hours' start they could, with their horses, leave any pursuing Indians well behind.

Still, Ree assured himself more than once flight would be the last thing he would recommend or think of. He declared it might be that Lone-Elk was more than a match for him, but the Seneca would have to prove it, and meanwhile the game he had commenced was one at which two could play.

Much thinking of all that had occurred and trying in vain to reason out the inward meaning of it all drove Kingdom to his bunk, completely worn out. With a determination, whose strength was one of his characteristics, he succeeded in putting his difficulties from him for the time, and soon soundly slept.

When the moon had risen, when the firelight in the cabin no longer brightly burned, when all the clearing was hushed and silent, Lone-Elk gave utterance to a contemptuous, disgusted "Ugh!"

Fishing Bird, alert and faithful every moment, heard the sound and noted with exquisite satisfaction the disappointment and chagrin the Seneca's tone expressed. As Lone-Elk turned and moved stealthily, as his habit was, deeper into the woods, and in the direction of the Delaware town, he followed. Elation over the toppling of Lone-Elk's hopes after all the toil and trouble with which he had followed the Paleface youth filled his heart. Dejected and sour must the Seneca go back to the village again. The thought that he, also, must make the weary journey and that he, also, had had but his labor for his pains, did not come to him. His conscience commended him for what he had done and the hardship of it all was only play.

It happened, however, that the generous Fishing Bird arrived at his conclusions quite too hastily. Satisfied that Lone-Elk was returning to the village, he gave little further heed to the Seneca's movements. Having allowed the latter a long start, he was content to go on slowly, taking pains only that he should not come upon the other unawares, or be likewise surprised himself.

When the morning broke on the village of the Delawares the Seneca was not there. Fishing Bird was the first to observe his absence. He had been away from the time the council closed the day before, some of the young braves said. They feared Lone-Elk, but they also admired him for his strength and his knowledge, and being much given to watching all his movements, they had noticed his absence from the first.

Alarmed and much provoked with himself, the Indian friend of the two young white men spent an anxious day. He feared at any moment to see the Seneca come striding proudly among the lodges, as his custom was, dangling the scalp of Little Paleface in such a way that none would fail to see it. Again and again he was tempted to visit the cabin of the boys, but dreaded to do so lest his presence there be discovered and result in so much of suspicion being aroused that his usefulness in the lads' interests would be ended.

All day Fishing Bird moved idly about or sat silently in his lodge, showing neither by word or look or action the anxiety he felt, though it increased more and more as the afternoon waned and Lone-Elk continued absent. But at last his long watch ended. Just at sunset the Seneca came wearily into the village. At his belt hung two pouches, both of which seemed heavy. One of them he gave to a group of squaws who were tending the boiling of a great pot of beans. It contained salt. The other he carried to Captain Pipe and without a word emptied its contents upon a bearskin at the chief's feet.

"More bullets!"

"More bullets, more lead, Chief Hopocon," the Seneca answered, using the Delaware's Indian name, "more lead for the brave warriors of the Delawares."

CHAPTER XI – THE HIDDEN TOMAHAWK

A most uncomfortable feeling of horror and astonishment held John Jerome speechless and motionless as he looked on the appalling scene which his moving of the brush heap had revealed. For the time all his senses seemed to desert him and, acting on an impulse of utter dismay, he hastily drew the bulk of the brush pile over the bodies again and hurried away.

As if he would find a refuge there, John hastened to the rude shelter where he had spent the night and where a few coals, still bright and warm, seemed to radiate a protecting air about the lonely spot.

All thoughts and actions are influenced more or less by one's surroundings, and being in the presence of that which suggested comfort and tranquillity, the startled boy was able presently to regain his composure somewhat. But if ever John desired the company of Ree Kingdom, and felt the need of his aid and counsel, he did now.

If only his own inclinations were to have been consulted, Jerome would have set out for home at as lively a pace as possible. Only the thought of the questions Ree would ask, and which he would be unable to answer, stood in his way. He could easily assure himself that, so far as his own curiosity was concerned, he had no wish to look again upon the awful objects the brush covered. Yet it would not do to go back to Kingdom with practically no definite information.

Mustering all the resolution he could, therefore, John returned to the dreadful spot, walking with great caution and with many anxious glances in all directions. He knew that the two bodies must have been placed where he had found them at least two or three days earlier, yet he was haunted by the feeling that the murderers were hiding close by. He rather expected, indeed, that the next moment they would jump out and seize him.

In this state of mind it required all the courage he could command to take hold of the lower portions of the matted mass of brush and drag the whole heap to one side; but he did it, and quickly then, lest his nerve fail him before the task was done, he examined both the corpses.

One was that of a man of about thirty years, dressed in homespun clothes and having in general appearance the unmistakable marks of the frontier about him. The hair was red and the face and hands showed many freckles despite the discoloration which had taken place.

The other body had been in life a robust giant of a fellow, perhaps twenty-two years old, with long, thick black hair, and a short, stubby growth of beard upon his face. The finer texture of the clothing and the style of the garments denoted a man from the east, one who was not ordinarily a hunter or a woodsman.

Both men had been shot—one from the side, for the bullet had entered his temple; the other undoubtedly from behind. The wound was hardly noticeable but the bullet had seemingly shattered the spinal column.

No valuables, no papers, no arms, absolutely nothing was there, so far as John could find, on or near either of the bodies which would furnish any clew to their identity. Powder horns, knives and all things of the kind usually carried by men in the woods had been taken away. The further fact that the dead had been scalped, as well as robbed, convinced John that Indians had done the deed. He did not linger long, however, to speculate upon the question. Placing the covering of brush over the bodies again, he literally fled from the spot, nor did he slacken his speed to a rapid walk until he had left the cause of his alarm a full mile behind.

Unnerved and depressed as he was, John entirely forgot the danger which confronted him in his accustomed haunts, and constantly thought of but one thing, which was that he must see Kingdom and tell him of the terrible discovery without a moment's delay.

"I'll keep going all night; no rest for me now," he told himself, and yet what he meant to do or what he supposed Ree would be able to do concerning the matter uppermost in his mind, he would not have been able to say.

Night came on. Poor Jerome had eaten nothing since morning and his fatigue was great. His mind was calmer now, and he felt the uselessness of going on without rest or food. Beside a great log where the wind had drifted the freshly fallen leaves he sat down, therefore, and ate the little meat he had remaining. It was rather comfortable here, he thought — almost any resting place would seem so after such a day as he had had — and he wrapped his blanket about him and lay down. The next day he would be back to the rocky ledges and the friendly hollow poplar again. By Monday morning, if not before, he would see Kingdom, that is, if nothing had befallen him. After what he had seen at the "lick" he would not be surprised to hear of more dreadful things.

How greatly both he and Ree had trusted the Indians, he reflected. Now if he could but find Kingdom safe and sound, and they both could get away to Fort Pitt or any place of safety, he would ask nothing more. But no, on second thought, he would ask yet one thing. It would be the privilege of joining Gen. Wayne's army and taking up arms against the savages in any campaign the white military would conduct.

And so thinking, John Jerome fell asleep.

It was a crisp, bright, fall night. Return Kingdom had eaten his supper quite dejectedly after spending the whole day watching for the coming of Lone-Elk or others of the Indians, while making scarcely more than a pretense of being busy husking corn. He was glad that John would soon return. While he had no thought of deserting the cabin and the clearing, he would feel much more comfortable to have Jerome somewhere near. True, he could see but little of him until Lone-Elk's accusation was effectually disposed of, but there would at least be some one with whom he could discuss the situation, some one sharing with him the news of each day's developments and the plans for future action.

In a brown study Ree sat before the fireplace. Then an Indian yell, fierce and loud—a yell which was more of a war-whoop than he was glad to hear—brought him quickly to his feet. Seizing his rifle, he opened a loophole in the wall in a corner where the light was dim, and looked out. A party of savages was approaching. The Indians moved in single file, making no effort to conceal their numbers, and seeming to be bent on no particular mischief.

Reassured by his observations, Kingdom opened the door while the redskins were yet but half way up the hill and, putting on an appearance of unconcern, called out to know who was disturbing the night with such a racket.

"The Delawares have come to demand the Little Paleface," the voice of Lone-Elk rose in response.

"You mean the Seneca has come," Kingdom boldly answered. "It is he who demands that one who was never anything but the friend of the Delawares shall be punished for a crime that is not his."

By this time the Indians were close about the cabin door.

"Come in, friends," Kingdom continued, his voice taking on a more cordial tone. "I suppose you have come to look for Little Paleface, but he is not here nor has he been for many days."

"Witches come or witches go. Like the wind they are here but they are gone. Let the Delawares see."

These words from Lone-Elk set all the party to looking about in careful search. No crevice was too small to escape their investigations. They seemed to think the so-called witch might hide himself in a space not large enough to admit a hand, and peered into every chink and corner.

It developed later that the savages were looking more for evidence of witchcraft than for the alleged witch himself. Still nothing was discovered.

"Brothers, hearken to Lone-Elk," the Seneca cried presently. "We remember the great crow which sat so long upon the gathered corn. Look, then, where the corn was. Witches take strange forms but they leave marks behind, if the Delawares can find them."

In a body the reckless party of braves the Seneca had brought rushed toward the cornfield. Only one loitered in the rear and he was Fishing Bird.

Lone-Elk was in advance. Even while he spoke, he was leading the way, and as if he had marked the spot well, he went directly to the shock of corn on which the vagrant crow was perched the day the Indians watched in vain for John Jerome while he slyly peeked out at them from the cabin loft.

"Tear down the corn! See what can be found!" the Seneca cried, and with a violent jerk laid the shock of fodder over upon the ground.

"Ugh!"

The savage who spoke was an evil-looking fellow and one of Lone-Elk's warmest followers. Even as his exclamations were made, he seized a heavy stone tomahawk, which lay on the ground where the shock of corn had been, and held it up for all to behold.

Lone-Elk shrugged his shoulders significantly and called all the Indians together. Here, he declared, was the identical hatchet which had slain Big Buffalo. And see the dark stains upon it! Even in the moonlight did they show red with the blood of the dead warrior.

With talk of this kind the anger of the Delawares was inflamed. Most of them now believed implicitly the charges of witchcraft Lone-Elk had made, and a few words from him would be sufficient to cause an immediate attack to be made upon Ree and the cabin.

Kingdom saw his danger. He knew as well as if he had seen the thing done that Lone-Elk had concealed the tomahawk beneath the shock of corn, but what could he do or say? If only Fishing Bird would tell what he had seen after following the Seneca to the white boys' clearing, it might be enough to turn the sentiment of the Indians another way. They would see that they were being trifled with and their ignorance played upon by one who was not trusted even by his own tribe. The whole trouble might be settled at once.

But Fishing Bird did not speak and Kingdom would not betray the friendly fellow's confidence, though his very life depended upon it. Still he made light of the discovery of the tomahawk and told Lone-Elk to his face that he knew perfectly well who hid the hatchet in the corn.

So bold was Ree, indeed, in making this and other accusations against the Seneca that the latter would have made an end of the young white man then and there but for his fear of Captain Pipe. As it was, he satisfied himself with inflaming the Delawares against Ree, as well as against the "Paleface witch," and undoubtedly hoped in secret that some of the more reckless ones would set fire to the cabin, or even kill its owner. So long as he could tell their chief that the Delawares themselves, not he, had committed the outrage and violated the promise made the young Paleface, he could wish nothing better.

Kingdom owed it to Fishing Bird and two or three others, but to Fishing Bird most of all, that the exciting talk of the Seneca resulted in no immediate harm to him. The counsel of these Indians was not of the loud and angry manner of Lone-Elk's bitter speeches, but to the contrary, quiet and persuasive.

"The Delawares will bide their time. They will do nothing rash because Lone-Elk seeks with talk to drive them to madness. Can it be the Seneca has some reason that we know not of for desiring the trouble he seeks to cause?"

With many quiet remarks of this character, spoken in the Indian tongue, Fishing Bird moved among the excited braves and warriors, and more than one, chancing to hear his low spoken words, stopped in the midst of his shouting and threatening demonstrations to consider if what Fishing Bird said was not pretty wholesome counsel after all.

Through all the uproar and while the savages ran here and there, shrieking and excited, upsetting the shocks of corn and doing much other annoying damage, bent on finding more hidden tomahawks or other evidence of witchcraft, Kingdom stood in the cabin doorway. He could close and bar the door in a second if it should be necessary to do so, he knew; but until that time came he meant to give none of the Delawares, much less Lone-Elk, any cause for believing that he was in any manner frightened or at all seriously disturbed.

When it became apparent that nothing more was to be discovered, the few Indians who had not already taken heed of the words of Fishing Bird quieted down and seeing that they would commit no greater or further violence, the Seneca summoned all to gather round him. Close to the cabin he led the band, and not knowing what the treacherous rascal might have in mind, Kingdom gripped his rifle closer and even slung it up to a position over his arm in which he could make quick use of the weapon.

"The White Fox was to give himself as a hostage for the delivery of the Paleface witch to the Delawares," Lone-Elk cried to the Indians who gathered round him. "If the one that is called Little Paleface is not a witch and did not kill Big Buffalo with his witch's hatchet, let the White Fox say where the Little Paleface is, and come now as a hostage to the great chief, Hopocon, till the murderer of Big Buffalo is found."

"Even as the Great Spirit knows that Little Paleface did not kill Big Buffalo, so does Lone-Elk know it. He knows it as well as he knows how came that hatchet hidden in the corn," Kingdom answered loudly, and with a tone of solemn certainty that could not escape the Indians' notice. "And I, whom the Delawares call White Fox; I, who have been their friend and enjoyed their friendship in return until Lone-Elk came among you, now call upon all who are here, and all the people of Captain Pipe's town, to witness this statement—that if harm comes to Little Paleface or to me, every Delaware will regret it;-that the Great Spirit hears me when I say that in the end we all shall know by whose hand Big Buffalo was killed, and we shall see that it was not by witchcraft that he died."

"Much talk! A young buck's much big talk!" grunted Lone-Elk contemptuously in English; but that Kingdom's solemn words and manner had much impressed a majority of the Indians the young pioneer himself well knew, and the Seneca must have seen it also. At any rate he started off toward the Delaware town, swinging the blood-stained tomahawk over his shoulder as he went. One by one the others followed.

CHAPTER XII — KINGDOM ALSO MAKES A DISCOVERY

Return Kingdom firmly believed that sooner or later the true cause and manner of Big Buffalo's death must become known. It must be so, he argued within himself. There had been times in history when the innocent had suffered for the guilty, but the saying, "murder will out," had been proved a true one always. Ree pinned his faith to it now. He did not so much as question how the truth would become known. In unseeing confidence he was willing to risk anything on his firm conviction that right must win and would win in the end, however slight the chance might seem.

And it is not too much to say, just here, that in after time it came to pass that all that Kingdom believed would happen, did happen; still, could he have looked forward to, and have seen the end, as he stood lonesome and nervous in the cabin door when the last of the Indians, — even Fishing Bird, — had departed, there would have been no more astonished young man in America that night.

Hopeful that Fishing Bird would come back for a talk with him when the Indians had passed into the woods and he could drop behind without his absence being noticed, Kingdom left the door ajar and sat for a long time before the smoldering embers of his fire. It was Saturday night, he reflected. There would be no work tomorrow, no hunting, no trapping. He would set off on foot, as if going for a stroll in the woods, and by traveling two sides of a triangle come at last to the old hollow whitewood and there wait for the coming of John. If the latter had made particularly good progress and had not loitered about the "big lick" too long, he should be arriving by early afternoon. Perhaps he had returned even now.

"And I'll wager a pair of boots that he'll be hungry enough, too!" Kingdom said to himself as he concluded his reflections; and being reminded by this that he was hungry, he ate some cold roasted venison, then looked out of the door once more for Fishing Bird, before creeping into bed.

Believing now that he had not been watched or followed after leaving the Indian town on the day of the council, Return concluded that Lone-Elk was too busy with his own affairs to spend a great deal of time spying about the clearing. Yet when he started from the cabin the following morning he traveled in a direction at right angles with that in which he wished to go, and moved very cautiously. He did not doubt that the Indians were searching for John Jerome, but concerning his own movements he reasoned that he would not be suspected of intending to go far, since he went on foot. And at the worst, if he found himself followed, he could gradually make his way home, leaving the spies no wiser than before.

For a considerable distance Kingdom walked along the old trail to the east as if he were but strolling through the woods. The day was bright and sunny and except for the raw north wind would have been of an ideal Indian summer type. Overhead great flocks of crows were cawing lustily. Eddies of the breeze whirled leaves here and there, and all in all there were many sounds abroad to drown the noise of footfalls on the soft mold and the leafy carpet of the forest.

For two miles or more Kingdom followed the irregular course of the eastward trail. Now he would turn abruptly to the north, he thought, and soon be safe from discovery in the unmarked depths of the woods. He paused and listened for a moment before leaving the path.

Hark! The sound of footfalls soft as a cat's, but coming steadily nearer, reached the boy's ears. He was followed.

Quick as the thought which flashed across his brain, and without noise, Kingdom stepped from the beaten trail and crouched behind a little knoll thickly overgrown with low bushes. Now if his pursuer, whoever he might be, would but pass on, he could effectually throw him off the scent before the latter discovered that his game had left the traveled path and so eluded him.

The breathless interest with which Ree listened to the approach of the stealthy footfalls can more easily be imagined than described. He had little doubt that it was Lone-Elk who was, dogging his movements. But soon he would know for certain. Whoever it was he would pass within a yard of the knoll and the brush which screened him. Would he go on by, and how far would he be likely to go before discovering that he had missed the course?

The pursuer came quickly forward. His body was bent in an eager attitude of listening and careful watchfulness, as if he would look far ahead despite the brush and trees and the low boughs which shut out his view. A hound, following a scent so faint that he might at any moment lose it, could not have been more intent or more keenly in earnest.

Listening and watching with bated breath, Kingdom saw the fellow approach and steal quickly on. It was Lone-Elk.

Hardly had the Seneca passed the spot of Kingdom's concealment, however, than he stopped, and stooping down, placed his ear to the ground. He seemed perplexed and uncertain. For several seconds he intently listened. But at last, still doubtful apparently, but anxious lest he was allowing himself to fall too far behind, he continued on, rather faster than before.

In spite of the danger of his position, Kingdom could scarcely suppress an audible chuckle as he saw Lone-Elk outwitted; but he realized that he "laughs best who laughs last," and without losing an instant in self-congratulation he rose and stepped into the path again. The Seneca had passed out of sight. "And so goodbye to you for this time," the boy thought, as he listened carefully and heard nothing, then exerting himself to the utmost to move quietly, he sped back along the path in the direction from which he had come.

For a quarter of a mile Ree continued his flight, then with a sudden broad leap left the path and traveled more moderately toward the north and west. At every step through the unbroken woods he sought to avoid leaving any trail which could be followed. Too cautious and too wise to risk going straight forward to the hollow poplar, although he had every reason to believe he had completely eluded the Seneca, Kingdom loitered here and there and traveled quite a zig-zag course.

By degrees, however, he came to the vicinity he sought and, to assure himself that he was not now watched, he sat down on a big boulder to rest and listen. As he waited he felt that somehow his sense of satisfaction in having given Lone-Elk the slip was disappearing. Why was it? Had he "counted his chickens before they were hatched," after all? The feeling grew on him that he was not alone, that somewhere near there were eyes which were on him constantly.

It is a dreadful sensation to feel that you are spied upon. Even to imagine that some one is secretly watching every breath you take, gazing intently, as if to read your very thoughts, is painful. To Kingdom, with the conviction growing in his mind that Lone-Elk had picked up his trail and had at no time been far behind him, the feeling was almost enough to unnerve him.

There was one way to determine whether this new trouble was real or imaginary, Kingdom told himself, and soon made use of it. Rising quickly, he started off at a brisk pace, looking neither to right nor left. Then, setting himself to catch the slightest sound, he suddenly stopped. A thrill ran through him. The noise he heard was unmistakable. There was a distinct rustling among the leaves. It stopped an instant after he did.

Ree well knew the wonderful power many of the Indians had for following others in the woods, especially along unbeaten trails, without revealing themselves. He knew, too, that Lone-Elk of all others was most certain to be adept in such practices. To go on to the meeting place agreed upon with John would be, therefore, the height of foolishness.

Twice again Ree stopped to harken for his pursuer's footsteps. Once he was certain be heard them. The other time he was sure he heard nothing; but when he walked back along his own trail a little way, he was conscious of a shadow having moved among the trees in the distance, though he saw nothing more tangible.

Ree's first impulse was to go in pursuit of the Seneca; for he did not question the identity of the spy, but thinking better of it, he resolved slowly to change his course so as to go at no time near the old poplar. He would reach the river after a time and, following its banks, eventually return to the cabin. A grievous disappointment it was to give up the meeting with John, but there was no help for it if that young gentleman's scalp was to be kept in safety where nature placed it.

Constant as his own shadow always, Kingdom felt the Seneca's presence steadily near him. He did not need to look around. He did not need to pause or listen. In his heart he knew the redskin was close by, as well as if they were walking side by side. He was getting into the rough and broken country now, just back from the river valley. Soon he would alter his course again to head more directly toward home.

Thus was Ree thinking when in a little gully, nearly bidden by high, precipitous banks, he suddenly beheld the ashes of a campfire and, spread upon a few broad strips of bark, something white and glistening. It couldn't be snow. There had been none. It was salt spread out to dry.

Like a flash the thought came to Ree and with it the certain conviction that John Jerome was just out of sight in the sheltered place below, or gone, perhaps, to keep the appointment at the old poplar.

Instantly Kingdom changed his course. His whole effort now was to keep the Seneca from seeing what he had seen. He dared not run, lest he create suspicion in Lone-Elk's mind; but he quickened his pace and held to a direction which he hoped would result in the Indian, intent only on watching him, cutting off the sharp corner he had turned and so not approaching as near to the edge of the bluff as he had done.

In his thoughts Ree scolded John Jerome sharply. What did the boy mean, anyway, by so exposing himself? What was the drying of a little salt from the "big lick" as compared to his own safety? And at a time when his very life was at stake!

At last the river was reached. Lone-Elk was still coming on behind. There could be no doubt of it. Repeatedly Kingdom had heard the gravel under his feet as the Seneca clambered down the steep banks after him.

What a change his chance discovery of John's camp had caused, Ree thought. A little while ago he was distressed because the Indian was always coming after him. Now he would be worried, indeed, should he find that the fellow had discontinued the pursuit. If the Seneca should give up the chase now it could mean but one thing—that he, too, had seen the camping place and was going there in search of more immediate results than his present labor promised.

A variety of tactics did Ree adopt to keep the pursuing Indian interested in watching him. Often did he pause and pretend to look all about with the greatest caution, and to listen closely, as if he had come at last to the very place which he had set out to reach. Again, he would suddenly hurry forward among the trees, or dart in here or there amidst the bushes, as though trying to escape the observation of anyone who might be near.

Up to the cabin was the game played. Only when the clearing, was reached did it end. Tired, alarmed, and more or less out of spirits, as he reckoned the extent of time wasted—a large part of the day—Kingdom sat down on a shock of corn which the Delawares had upset the night before. As he did so, he caught sight of the Indian for the first time since morning. The Seneca was moving silently from tree to tree, but apparently watching all that the white boy did.

Moved by the grim humor of the long, unavailing chase he had led the redskin, Kingdom called out to the fellow:

"Hi, there, Lone-Elk, haven't you had enough of that sort of thing for one day?"

In an instant the savage stepped into the clearing.

"Paleface is a fool," he spoke in English, and raised his rifle menacingly.

88

"Put up that gun, Lone-Elk, and come sit down here! Come, sit down, and let's talk matters over just by ourselves," Kingdom returned in a friendly tone. The ugly manner of the Indian really alarmed him, but he took this way of concealing the fact; and, moreover, if the Seneca could be persuaded to discuss their differences just between themselves, much might be accomplished.

With a contemptuous "Ugh!" Lone-Elk threw his rifle over his arm again. But instead of accepting Kingdom's invitation, he turned into the woods and was soon gone from sight.

Still Kingdom remained sitting on the bundle of fodder. He was thinking of John Jerome and the camp in the gully near the river. The more he reflected, the more inclined he was to believe that it was not John's camp that he had discovered. How could John have brought salt from the "lick?" He had not had time enough to make any. That he had obtained it of some one whom he found there was possible, but hardly likely. But, on the other hand, if the camp was not John Jerome's, whose in the world was it? Who was spreading salt to dry in the depths of the Ohio wilderness?

CHAPTER XIII — THE SENECA OUTWITTED

So long as he believed Lone-Elk to be near the clearing, Ree was little better than a prisoner, so far as going to find John Jerome was concerned; and as he realized that the Seneca might prolong his stay indefinitely, he turned his thoughts to some plan by which he might be rid of the fellow. He had no intention of letting Lone-Elk suspect what was in his mind, however. On the contrary, he would endure a great deal rather than give the Indian the satisfaction of knowing how greatly he desired to be alone.

Sauntering leisurely to the cabin, Kingdom sat in the doorway to eat and drink, for he was still warm with the vigorous exercise of the forenoon. Then he fed the horses and for a time busied himself about the stable. Constantly was he alert to discover whether Lone-Elk was still in the vicinity, and as he watched through a crack from inside the barn, he several times saw the Indian. The unyielding savage was moving uneasily from point to point, but his eyes were turned always in the direction of the cabin, and his manner seemed to express a determination to look nowhere else for a long time to come.

Surely it was enough to bring despair to anyone, Kingdom told himself. Then the thought came to him that maybe Lone-Elk was despairing quite as much as he. He recalled a rule that good old Captain Bowen had once laid down for him when he and John were planning their first trip west — "Don't give up. When you are just about done for and you think you can't hold out a second longer, just keep your hold the stronger; for you can depend on it that the other fellow is more or less winded if you are, and you don't know but he is more."

Gaining encouragement in such reflections, Kingdom set his teeth and a smile which was not pleasant to see came to his lips. Very quietly and naturally, however, he carried a bucket of fresh water up from the river and went into the cabin and sat down. If he could do nothing else, he would slip through the barn and get into the woods in the darkness. He could lie by in some secluded place until morning and for Lone-Elk to find him, after he had obtained such a start, would be more than even that determined redskin was likely to undertake.

The shadows lengthened. With the thought of slipping away in the darkness in mind, Kingdom let the fire die down and from loopholes constantly watched the clearing to make certain the Seneca did not approach the buildings and so be able to prevent his leaving.

Slowly the gathering darkness deepened. It closed around the little log house and stump-dotted open space in the forest's fastnesses. It closed around Lone-Elk, the Seneca, unrelenting and vigilant. But it closed around another, too, who watched the cabin on the bluff with patience and with perseverance quite equal to the Indian's.

When John Jerome awoke from the deep sleep into which he fell beside the log that protected him not only from the night wind but from sight as well, if by any chance Indians or others should be passing, he stirred uneasily and at last sat up. A yelp and a sudden rustling of the leaves accompanied his movement. More startled than frightened, John leaped to his feet. Two pairs of eyes shone yellowish-green in the darkness, and a hungry growl came from the same direction.

"Scatter, you varmints!" cried the boy, and clubbing his gun, sprang toward the creatures.

The wolves retreated, but only a few steps. Again John leaped toward them and this time also sent a heavy, half-rotten limb from the old log flying after them. Made bold by hunger, however, the brutes only growled the more fiercely.

"Looks as if I'd have to give one of you a little lead," the boy remarked, and calmly sat down on the fallen tree trunk. Still he hesitated to shoot, disliking both to waste the powder and to attract attention toward himself. He was still rather nervous from the shock received at the "lick."

"Almost daylight, anyhow," John reflected. "I'll get an early start." He sat quiet, therefore, calmly eyeing the shining balls which gleamed at him until the first peep of light. Even then the wolves lingered near; but, paying little further attention to them, the lad set off at a rapid pace, once more on the homeward way and thankful for it.

Before the morning was far advanced Jerome found himself among familiar scenes. With boyish pleasure he greeted each fresh object that he recognized. A gnarled old oak, whose oddly twisted branches he had noticed more than once, seemed like an old friend. A tall stub of an ash, long since dead, but plainly marked by the claws of bears, was likewise a friendly landmark and he whispered, "Hello, there, you look natural!" as he might have done in greeting a fellow creature.

Making rapid progress now, for he hoped Ree would be waiting at the hollow whitewood, the returned explorer arrived in the vicinity of that rendezvous somewhat before noon. As his custom was, he made a wide circuit to reconnoiter before going to the tree itself, taking every step with care and keeping eyes wide open in all directions.

John did not expect to see anyone or to find anything unusual in thus spying out "the lay of the land." He never had found the coast otherwise than clear; still he had no intention of revealing the fine hiding place in the old poplar by lack of reasonable prudence and so walked guardedly and with every sense alert. Something like a shadow moved among the trees and bushes a hundred yards ahead. It might be only a bird, or a squirrel or some larger animal, but John sheltered himself behind a tree and looked again more carefully.

"Lone-Elk!"

The name he thought, but did not utter, and the sight of its owner sent a thrill through Little Paleface that made him hold his breath. The Indian was moving through the woods with an easy, natural stealth, so light, so silent, that if he had had the power of making himself all but invisible it could not have seemed more wonderful.

John's first thought was that the Seneca was looking for him; but he quickly saw that this could not be, for his eyes were turned steadily and keenly in another direction.

"The lead mine! He is stealing up to the secret lead mine just like a ghost!" was the boy's second mental exclamation.

But again John was wrong, as the reader will have guessed. It was upon Return Kingdom that the Indian had his eyes, and it was fortunate indeed for Little Paleface that the Seneca was too occupied in that direction to look in any other; for so intensely interested did the lad become in watching the creature's cat-like movements that he stood fairly in the open, an object of easy discovery had his presence been suspected.

The temptation came to John to shoot his accuser down. Had he not the right to kill one who at sight would kill him? he asked himself; and a half minute later, when he found that it was his bosom friend that the redskin was so secretly pursuing, he was doubly-tempted to make an end of him. One bullet would do it. One bullet would settle this whole miserable witchcraft business. But how? What good would it do to have Lone-Elk out of the way if it became known that the "witch" was his slayer?

Then John saw, or thought he saw, that Kingdom knew he was followed. The whole truth came to him. Ree had set out to go to the whitewood but, being tracked by the Indian, had purposely refrained from going there.

Resolving to keep Lone-Elk in sight to give Kingdom any assistance he could, should the actions of the Indian become seriously threatening, John followed after them. He allowed between himself and the Seneca as great a distance as was possible, still keeping him in view, but so swift and silent were the fellow's movements that it was a puzzle for the eye to follow him.

With increasing interest in the mysterious game his friend and the Indian were playing, John did not at once realize that, after one sharp turn he had made, Ree was headed homeward. When he did make this discovery, however, it was only to decide that he would go, too, and thus was presented in the wilderness depths the odd picture of one person being unrelentingly trailed by another, who, in turn, was watched and followed by a third.

But even stranger things the unbounded woods of the early days full often witnessed. Stranger dreams have never come to man than were many of the realities of life in the wilds of the middle west a hundred and odd years ago.

While from one point at the clearing's edge Lone-Elk unceasingly bent his eyes upon the little log house on the bluff, John Jerome did likewise from another. John, however, had two objects to keep within his scrutiny. One, and the most important one, was the Seneca. Still he had ample opportunity to see what Ree was doing, and with particular interest he watched his chum sit eating and drinking in the doorway.

"And here I am, most starved, within sight of him!" the weary boy reflected. "Just wait till it's dark, you lonely old Elk you, and if you don't do something then, I will!"

An hour had passed since night closed in. Return Kingdom still watched from loopholes, wondering in vain, looking in vain, to know what the Seneca's nocturnal tactics would be. No sign of the Indian had he seen since darkness shut out the view across the clearing.

What was that noise? Ree started violently. The horses moved as if some one had come in the barn. In another second his ear was at a crack in the wall between the lean-to stable and the cabin, and he knew that something besides the horses was stealthily moving—yes, moving toward him; he heard it plainly now. What could that miserable, sneaking, malicious Indian be up to now! And then a whisper—

"Oh, Ree!"

"Blessed stars, John!" was the startled, whispered answer. "How did you come here? Don't you know Lone-Elk is watching the house this very minute?"

But nevertheless it was with a feeling of much relief and real pleasure that, when Jerome had whispered back, "Well, I guess I do," Ree told him to creep in through the "cat-hole," while he himself noiselessly double-barred the cabin door.

"Why, you had me scared into a catnip fit," said Kingdom, still whispering, as he felt about in the darkness for John's hand.

"Did I? But say, do you know it's snowing? And how I'm to get away again, now that I'm here, without making a trail that a blind man could follow, I'm blest if I can tell."

"Never mind that now, old chap," was the hopeful answer. "Rest yourself and I'll see what I can lay hands on for you to eat. I've got a few things to tell you after awhile."

"Things to tell, Ree? Cracky, so have I!"

And Lone-Elk, sullen and ugly, determined and relentless, still watched the cabin with unremitting perseverance from the deeper shadows of the woodpile at the clearing's edge.

CHAPTER XIV – THE MYSTERIOUS CAMP IN THE GULLY

"Honestly, my neck's out of joint, looking around trees all day," John declared. But he was so light-hearted, so glad to be home again, that he fairly giggled as he spoke.

"Faith! I'm glad you're here, unhealthy as it is for you," Kingdom answered. "What with Lone-Elk always just over my shoulder, and now with the snow on the ground, I don't know how I'd ever have managed to get to you in the woods!" And so the boys fell to telling each other all that each had been doing and all that had happened since their last meeting.

Kingdom showed the greatest interest in the discovery of the bodies of the two men whom John had found dead under the brush heap at the salt springs. He inquired for every shred of information possible for John to give him, and tried his best to determine whether the murder had been committed by Indians or white men. If it was done by white persons, he declared, the slayer or slayers had at any rate tried to make it appear that Indians were the guilty ones. The carrying off the scalps of the dead and removing all valuables from the bodies indicated this.

"Still, I don't see what it signifies, or how it makes any great difference to us, one way or another," said John, as Ree intimated that he would have looked into the matter more thoroughly had it been he who made the discovery.

"Why, of course you do, John! Just think a minute! I've told you about seeing that camp in the little hollow and the salt spread out to dry. Now, then, where did that salt come from if not from the big 'lick'? You mark my word that when we find out whose camping place that is, or was, we will know pretty well who did that killing. What we ought to do is to carry the whole story to Wayne's men or to Fort Pitt; but it wouldn't do any good to go there merely telling that we had found a couple of men dead. Persons are found dead along the border, somewhere, every day in the year. But if we could go to Wayne, or anyone else, and show them that the murderers were white robbers, and not simply sneaking redskins, there would be more of a chance to call somebody to account."

"That's so," John answered rather thoughtfully, yet in a way which showed Ree that he did not quite understand.

"Why, certainly!" Kingdom exclaimed somewhat warmly. "If the camp I saw was the camp of the murderers, who is it likely that they are? British! That's what! British from Detroit, over in this part of the woods for no good purpose—spying around Fort Pitt or stirring the Indians up to hostilities! And that camp I saw was a white man's camp! Indians don't care much about salt to begin with, and in the second place what white men would be traveling in this direction and carrying salt with them but some one headed for Detroit or some other settlement off that way?"

But having reached a conclusion that Indians, and no one else, were responsible for the two dead bodies beneath the brush pile, John could not easily get the notion out of his mind, and his interest in Kingdom's speculations was therefore much less than ordinarily it would have been.

On the other hand Ree pieced together every scrap of evidence he could find—the stained glove that John had picked up, the indications he noticed that others had journeyed toward the "lick" from the west, and the certainty his own find presented that some one had lately obtained salt, presumably from the springs, in quite considerable quantities.

Extremely tired and too drowsy, now that he was in the midst of warmth and comfort again, to think much of the danger of his position, John fell into a doze on his bunk while Kingdom still pondered upon the salt springs mystery. In the darkness Ree did not at once notice that Jerome was asleep. Later he made the discovery and it was quite like him that he covered his friend over with a bearskin, and set himself to watch till daybreak.

It was fairly light when John awoke. Ree had already been out and the tracks he found showed that Lone-Elk had abandoned his watch. He had gone some time after it stopped snowing in the night, but there was no knowing when he might return.

Although the fact did not occur to either of the two boys at the time, the coming of the snow was, under the circumstances, a blessing in disguise. For the Seneca, after watching vigilantly until nearly morning, and feeling confident that no one except Kingdom had entered the cabin, was equally sure that no one would do so now that the snow would at once reveal the trail. With this thought in mind he had quit his post and, so far as his own trail showed, had returned again to the town beside the lake.

The perfect quiet within the clearing, and the sense of comfort and greater security which Ree found in having companionship once more, permitted him to be persuaded to lie down for the sleep and rest he so greatly needed, while the younger of the lads did guard duty at the loopholes in the cabin wall. At the first sign of anyone approaching, it was agreed he should call Ree, then quickly conceal himself in the loft. Sooner than the boys expected, the worth of their plan was put to the test.

A party of seven Indians, Wyandots from the region of Sandusky, traveling up the river in canoes, landed that morning at the point where the river met the portage trail, near the cabin of the young Palefaces. As did most of the Indians for many miles around, they knew of the presence of the two venturesome white lads in the wilderness, and did not hesitate to stop for a warm bite to eat and to see what the Paleface brothers offered in the way of trade.

Little did the Wyandots guess as they drew near the cabin, however, the flurry their presence caused inside. A mere whisper from John awakened Ree. In a twinkling the latter sent Jerome climbing into the loft "like a scared rabbit into its hole," as he afterward expressed it, and pulling the little ladder up after him.

Kingdom greeted the visitors in his pleasantest manner. They spread their hands before the bright blaze in the big fireplace, and ate heartily of the meat he set before them. Nevertheless, when the strangers showed a disposition to look about rather more closely than seemed natural, even standing on tip-toe to peer into the loft, the lad grew decidedly uneasy.

As for John, he watched through a crack all that went on below with a great deal of interest, indeed. He was scarcely more than a foot above the heads of the taller Indians. The least sound from his direction would reach them and excite their suspicion.

Would the Wyandots never go?

Before they had been five minutes in the cabin Ree was wondering why they lingered so. Every second was magnified sixtyfold as he watched and waited, doing his best to appear perfectly at ease.

"Much skins up here," one swarthy young fellow with a single black and red feather in his hair remarked, and with his foot on a stool climbed partially into the loft.

"Oh, not many—you come down now, brother! You'll bring poles and all down on our heads," Ree answered, and quickly drawing the Wyandot down, placed the stool in a place where it would not be so readily available for such use again.

"Have the Wyandots any salt to trade for knives or cloth or anything else we have for them?" asked Kingdom, hoping to obtain information which might be valuable.

"No salt; Injuns got no salt. Paleface get big heap salt at big 'lick,'" answered the leader of the band. "Paleface over yonder—him have salt. Him trade, maybe."

"Where? Where over yonder do you mean?" Kingdom inquired, pretending to be little interested.

"Over yonder—down river. Him have camp piece back from river, yonder."

"Just one man, is it!" Ree asked.

"Ugh! two—leben—four—cuss! Injun don't know!" the Wyandot returned, and seeing that the redskin suspected that he was being "pumped," Ree changed the subject as naturally as he could.

Every moment that the Wyandots tarried the boy feared their next words would be to ask where John was. All the Indians knew there were two of the white boys, and that they were usually together. Had these travelers learned of the charge of witchcraft against Little Paleface? Kingdom dared not turn their thoughts in that direction by any words pertaining to the subject, and he was glad enough to say goodbye to them, at last, even though on this point he had gleaned no information.

There was no need for Kingdom to tell what had been said and done by the visitors when, after they were well out of sight, John came clambering down from the loft.

"I'm getting awful tired of being a witch, Ree," the latter began, peeping out of a loophole. "What in the world's the use of our staying here and living this way? I'm not complaining, old boy, you know I'm not; but this sort of thing is likely to last all winter. You can't find out how Big Buffalo was killed, and until you know, every mother's son of those Delawares swallow all that Lone-Elk tells them. So how's it going to end? Am I to jump and run like a whipped pup, all winter, every time we hear a noise?"

"Just you wait, my son," Kingdom answered, quite gaily. "We know that the Seneca's hold on Captain Pipe is his secret lead mine. Suppose we find that mine! Mr. Pipe will be glad to find out where it is. There! Now you see what I mean. You're just feeling a little cross because you had to stay out of sight. But here's another thing, John. We agree that we don't intend to let any one Indian chase us away from here; but we have some business on hand besides that. We've got to find out, if we can, who killed those men at the salt springs. With all the reason we have for believing that the murderers are camped out just about under our very noses, we're bound to look after them, especially if they're white men, and—well, you heard what the Wyandots said just two minutes ago. Don't you think, either, John," the

100

older lad concluded very soberly, "that I don't see the danger we are in. I see it big and strong all around us; but we've gone too far to turn back unless we have to. If we can come out ahead of Lone-Elk just once, there will be no danger of his ever troubling us again. Pipe and all the Delawares will be our solid friends for all time. We don't want to sacrifice all we have done here and the good start we've made, do we, John?"

Ree's last sentence was an appeal. Jerome might have argued against every other point, but not against that. "We'll stay here till water runs up hill, Ree, before we'll budge an inch except we want to," he declared with quiet emphasis. "So what are we going to do next?" he added.

"Wait till the snow's gone," Ree answered cheerily. "It's thawing fast now and by afternoon we can hunt up that camp where I saw the salt spread out. Until then we will have to watch out that Lone-Elk doesn't come prowling around again."

"Good thing it's all we have to do. It's enough to keep one man busy," John returned, and undoubtedly he was right; but nevertheless their labor was for nothing this time. The Seneca was not discovered, nor was there a single visitor to the neighborhood of the clearing.

Kingdom's prediction that the snow would soon be gone was quickly verified; for the wind having changed to the southwest, a rain came up by noon which completed the work of the sun very quickly.

Call to mind the most gloomy, misty, wet and altogether disagreeable fall day you can remember, and you will have a fair idea of the sort of afternoon on which John Jerome and Return Kingdom tramped cautiously through the woods in search of the camp of the suspected salt spring murderers. The gloom in the thicker portions of the forest was little short of actual darkness and the mist or fog became so dense, as time went on, that objects were indistinguishable at a distance of more than a few yards.

The secret nature of their expedition and Kingdom's oft expressed belief that the camp they sought was occupied by British traders, or even soldiers from about Detroit, caused both the boys to feel a great deal of importance attaching to their undertaking. Just what they expected to discover, however, or what they intended saying regarding the purpose of their visit, in case they found the birds in their nest, neither of the two could very well have told.

Time and its developments answer many questions and so were the questions confronting Ree and John disposed of a little later. Kingdom had little difficulty in leading the way to the camp he had so strangely discovered. His familiarity with the woods for miles around would have made any spot in the vicinity of the cabin easily located.

Favored by the mist and semi-darkness, the two boys readily approached very near to the edge of the little bluff from which they could look down upon the camp without danger of their presence being discovered. Then on hands and knees they went forward more cautiously.

The birds, were gone. The nest was there, just as Ree had seen it, except that the salt had been taken away; but the camp was unoccupied and the ruins of the campfire were cold and water-soaked.

With much curiosity the two young detectives inspected the deserted camp and its surroundings. Nothing could they find to indicate who its makers had been or whither they had gone. In vain did they examine the ground within a radius of several yards from the heap of dead ashes. They discovered not so much, as a footprint.

Compelled at last to give up their search in disappointment, the boys were about to climb out of the protected nook the bluff formed on three sides of the camp, when John observed a small pile of wood such as would be gathered for a campfire in the forest. It was partially covered with leaves and being a rod or two from the site of the camp had not sooner been noticed.

"It may mean that they're coming back and it may not," the lad remarked. As he spoke he saw Kingdom pick up something a few feet away and quietly put it in his pocket.

"At any rate they're gone," Ree answered. "We may as well go, too."

The boys climbed the ascent to the higher ground without further comment. When they had gone some distance John asked:

"What was it that you found, Ree? I thought I saw you pick something up."

"What do you think, John? It was a glove, the mate to that other one. What do you think of that?" was the low but earnest answer.

And while the boys hurried quietly through the woods, there emerged from a small cave, screened from view by sumac and other bushes, in the little ravine, a roughly dressed man who climbed the bluff and gazed after them.

CHAPTER XV — THE GIFT OF WHITE WAMPUM

The effect on the minds of the boys of the discovery Kingdom had made was much the same as if they had seen a ghost. A vague fear of something unexpressed and unknown took possession of them and they hastened through the misty, sodden forest as though expecting every minute to be pursued. Kingdom remarked about their apprehensiveness.

"We act like a couple of thieves," he declared, "the way we are hurrying to get away! But suppose we were seen hunting around that camp and it was noticed that I picked up this glove; it wouldn't be exactly healthy for us, I suppose? Still, it's not that that makes us both nervous and fidgety as a fox in a trap; but what is it?"

"I don't know about you, but I'm thinking of those two dead men under the brush pile; just can't help it;" said John. "The man that wore those gloves knows how the bodies came there, I'll bet a buckskin!"

"Of course," was the answer, "but that's just what I have suspected all along. The deuce of it now is to know what we're going to do about it."

The darkness was coming on most rapidly. The dark, gray clouds seemed to settle down to the very ground. In half an hour it would be quite impossible to find one's way safely through the woods, for not a breath of wind was stirring; there would be absolutely nothing by which to be guided.

Seeing the importance of quickly reaching the neighborhood of the clearing, Kingdom proposed that John seek shelter for the night in the old whitewood while he continued on to the cabin. They would meet again soon after daybreak in the morning.

Having had some such plan in mind when setting out from home, the boys had blankets and provisions with them, and Jerome readily agreed to Ree's suggestion.

As the hollow poplar was now not far away, they parted company at once. Kingdom promised to leave the cabin before daylight again, if he could do so without discovery, and to meet John at the whitewood for another visit to the camp in the gully.

"And you wait for me, whatever happens," Kingdom said in admonition. "I'll be worrying all night if I think you're prowling around by yourself."

"Worry fiddlesticks!" ejaculated the younger lad, with a laugh. "What if I were to be worried about you?"

So the good-byes were said and ten minutes later John was snugly settled in the protecting trunk of the big hollow tree, glad enough to rest after his long tramp.

Kingdom, meanwhile, was hurrying on at increased speed. He aimed to travel in a sort of semicircle so as to approach the cabin from a direction which would give no clue to the locality from which he had come. He had little doubt that Lone-Elk would be watching for him. Indeed, it was only the great probability that the Seneca would be prowling about the vicinity of the clearing that had made it seem necessary that he return home instead of spending the night with John. The boys wished to keep the Indian in ignorance of the fact that the "witch" was in the neighborhood at all. If they could succeed in this for a time, the redskins, Lone-Elk particularly, would conclude at last that search for the missing boy was useless.

The complete darkness, the thick, cold mist and utter silence which pervaded the clearing and made it seem certainly the most desolate place in the world as he entered it, would have depressed and frightened bolder hearts than Kingdom's. He hurried up the familiar path, and ascended the slope to the little log house with dread. A whinny came from the stable. What a welcome sound it was! And when, five minutes later, the blaze in the big fireplace was dispelling the shadows, it seemed also to dispel the dreadful feeling of vague fear and homesickness from Ree's mind. He was himself again.

Worn out with much work and little rest for two days, Kingdom retired early. He knew that the dispirited condition, which sapped his courage and destroyed his peace of mind and self-confidence, was due to his being completely tired out, and that sleep would make all the next day's problems seem easy by putting him in shape to meet them. And so thinking he fell asleep.

It was near midnight, Kingdom thought, though really much earlier, when he was awakened. Some one rapped at the door,—quietly, secretly. Again he heard it,—thump, thump!—two short, quick taps, sounding as if made with finger tips.

"John!" was Ree's first thought; and he was out of his bunk in a second.

"Who is it?" he asked in a low tone, before opening the door.

"Fishing Bird has something to tell white brother," came the answer in tones so guarded, that, filled with wonder and anxiety, Kingdom unbarred and opened the door in a trice.

Instantly the Indian entered and Ree closed the door again. He felt, rather than saw, that the redskin was bedraggled, wet, cold and weary. He drew the visitor to the fireplace and sat him down. Though covered with ashes, the warm bed of coals gave off a comfortable degree of heat, and while the Indian leaned over the warm hearth, his host, still wondering, brought him meat and a dish of hominy.

Fishing Bird ate heartily. As he was doing so, a tiny flame, which for a second blazed up above the ashes, showed that his condition was even worse than Ree had pictured it. From the soles of his worn-out moccasins to the top of the uncombed hair falling in coarse, untidy strings about his ears and down his back, he was very wet and very dirty.

"What news, Fishing Bird?" Ree asked, when he had dressed and the visitor had eaten all he wished. "I've been wanting to see you for many days."

"Ugh! Lone-Elk very bad!" the Indian replied, meditatively. "Fishing Bird watch him all day, watch him in the night, too. He goes many places, and don't go nowhere."

Kingdom repressed a smile. He guessed at once that his friend had been trying to follow the Seneca to the secret lead mine, and had only his labor to show for it. A moment later the Indian confirmed this supposition.

"Lone-Elk gone all day long and comes to the Delaware village in the night," Fishing Bird went on. "Lone-Elk brings no lead. Next morning — today — Lone-Elk goes again and Fishing Bird follows behind. Maybe Lone-Elk be going to where lead is; maybe going to watch young Palefaces. But him walk, walk, walk, all the time going on and on and never getting anywhere at all. Never looking back; never knowing Fishing Bird comes on behind, so Lone-Elk went here, went there, all day. Night came and in the dark Lone-Elk got away and Fishing Bird couldn't watch him any more."

"Maybe he was hunting for Little Paleface," Kingdom suggested.

"Lone-Elk bad — a mean, bad Seneca Indian!" the weary and disgusted Delaware made answer. "Now Fishing Bird will tell news he came for. White Fox knows how Lone-Elk found tomahawk in the corn — how Lone-Elk told that it was the witch's hatchet — same hatchet that killed Big Buffalo. So Lone-Elk hangs the tomahawk at the door of his lodge and says with that hatchet he will kill the witch that killed the Delaware warrior. One time, two times, three times, did tomahawk fall down when Lone-Elk had hung it up. One time Lone-Elk a little mad. Two times Lone-Elk pretty mad. Three times, when hatchet fall down, Lone-Elk heap much mad.

"Neoliaw tell Lone-Elk not to hang tomahawk up like that any more. Neoliaw knows much. No Delaware knows all things like Neoliaw; yet Lone-Elk holds his head high and asks if Neoliaw thinks the Seneca is but a squaw to be frightened by such talk."

The Indian paused. Much interested, Kingdom waited with impatience for him to continue, but at length asked:

"And what did the medicine-man of the Delawares say to that? What did Neohaw say?"

107

"Neohaw tell Lone-Elk never mind. Some day tomahawk have more blood on it than now. Maybe it be Seneca blood."

"Do the Delawares still believe all that Lone-Elk tells them about how Big Buffalo was killed by a witch, and believe that the witch was our friend, John?" Kingdom inquired.

Fishing Bird nodded. "White brother shall hear more," he said, a moment later, as if having decided to reveal something he had at first thought he would not tell. "Listen, White Fox. Lone-Elk knows where lead is. Lone-Elk is a mighty warrior. Hopocon, that you call Captain Pipe, wants Lone-Elk in the fighting that will come bime-by, and wants lead for Delawares, Chippewas, Wyandots,—all the Indians that will be in the fighting off yonder," waving his hand toward the west and north. "So Hopocon sends white wampum as presents to the Seneca tribe for squaw of the warrior Lone-Elk killed. Because Lone-Elk killed a warrior, White Fox knows, he can go back never to his own people. Only if the presents, sent by Hopocon, are taken by the squaw of the warrior that was killed, will Lone-Elk be free to go here, go there, like other Indians. Then Hopocon will make him a Delaware."

Ree did not know until now the history of the outcast Seneca. He had known that Lone-Elk was a fugitive, but never before more than suspected the reason. In a general way he understood the Indian custom that if the nearest relative of one who was murdered received and accepted from the murderer or his friends a present in token of regret and sorrow — usually white wampum — it meant that the crime was forgiven and fully wiped out.

He knew, also, that if such a present was refused by the relatives or friends of the dead, that it meant but one thing—that at the first opportunity they would have their revenge by taking the life of the murderer. The custom had prevailed among the Iroquois and many of the other Indians for generations. It was implicitly followed.

The refusal of the peace offering usually meant eternal unforgiveness. It meant the exile of the murderer from his own tribe and the villages of his fathers forever. It meant death whenever one or more of the friends of the person killed started out to seek vengeance, — death swift and certain — unless the murderer succeeded in escaping them; but, once on the trail, the avengers knew no pause, no rest, no hardship too great to be undertaken, until their mission was accomplished.

Instantly realizing the great importance of Fishing Bird's information, Ree asked him to go on and tell more of the Seneca's history.

The friendly Delaware, however, seemed to believe that he had told enough. Maybe he regretted that he had already been so confidential. He sought to speak of other things, therefore, until Kingdom asked point blank:

"Will the friends of the one whom Lone-Elk killed be likely to accept the presents that have been sent, Fishing Bird?"

The Delaware nodded decidedly in the affirmative at first, then shook his head. He didn't know and couldn't guess, he stated, what view the dead man's relatives would take of the matter. It was the usual thing to receive such presents and grant forgiveness. A great deal depended on the nature of the crime, and the details of the murder Lone-Elk had committed, Fishing Bird did not know, or if he did, he pretended ignorance.

He believed the Seneca had struck another down with a tomahawk, and had afterward hidden the hatchet near the Delaware town to which he had originally escaped, and whither he had again come after the battle with St. Clair's army. At least that was the story the squaws had whispered to one another. The warriors were too proud to take notice of such matters, especially since Lone-Elk, by his prowess, by his constant activity, and afterward by his knowing of the lead mine, had become a leader among them.

All this information Fishing Bird rather reluctantly imparted. He was very tired and just a little cross. In response to some further questioning he said, plainly showing his impatience:

"Fishing Bird has told the white brothers they must not stay here. Still it has done no good. Fishing Bird is the friend of the two young Palefaces, yet they must not ask of him what no Delaware can do."

"Come, Fishing Bird," Ree answered kindly, "we are not going to ask you to endanger yourself or any of your people on our account. We know and appreciate how much you have helped us, and but for one thing we would probably go away as you suggest. And now there is only one more question I want to ask you; then you must lie down and rest till morning. Does Fishing Bird know of any other Palefaces, besides White Fox and Little Paleface, who are in the woods here; any who have been getting salt somewhere?"

The Delaware had lost his spunky feeling entirely when he answered. He did not, he said, know of any other white persons in the woods anywhere about. He was quite sure there was none; for the Indians were very watchful now, lest Paleface spies come among them, and would be quite sure to discover any white persons who came near.

A little later Ree spread a blanket and some skins upon the floor and urged Fishing Bird to lie down; but instead, the Indian rose to go, nor could he be prevailed upon to remain. Thinking that perhaps he wished to be back to the village before the Seneca returned, Kingdom reluctantly opened the door for him, and he went forth into the cold and darkness, and the thick, raw mist swallowed him up immediately.

CHAPTER XVI — A MIDNIGHT SUPPER

Seated on a bed of dry leaves in the snug shelter of the old whitewood, John Jerome ate his supper. Kingdom had made fresh corn bread and hominy and roasted a whole quarter of a deer during his otherwise enforced idleness a couple of days earlier, and all these things were very much to John's taste. He enjoyed his supper so much, indeed, and felt so strong and hearty after he had eaten and rested for a time, that he crept out from his retreat and stood upright among the bushes concealing the hiding place.

It lacked a little of being totally dark. Except for the dense fog, or mist, it would still be almost daylight, John thought, as he looked about him. He didn't feel like lying down to sleep at once. No, he wouldn't either. He would go out just a little way beyond the thicket and see if he could not discover some sign of a campfire down in the gully. That pile of wood which he and Ree had found was not there for nothing. It meant that the camp was not permanently abandoned. At any rate, he would see what he could see.

With some such reflections, by way of excusing himself for doing what Kingdom had told him not to do, John made his way cautiously and slowly toward the protected valley and the mysterious camp there hidden. No light of any kind shone in that direction, however, and he reasoned with himself that it was useless to go further. Still, he thought, there could be no harm and no danger either when veiled by such a mist in going clear up to the edge of the bluff.

Even while making excuses to himself John was edging stealthily onward. Soon the brink of the steep descent was just before him. He could not see into the valley but his familiarity with the trees and general lay of the land assured him that he had to go only a little farther to obtain a view of the mysterious camping place.

In his eagerness the venturesome young man was quite forgetful of danger. Making scarcely an effort to conceal himself, indeed, he was pushing steadily forward when suddenly he was recalled to a realization of his carelessness in a manner he long remembered.

With one foot on a fallen log, in the act of rising up to step quietly down on the other side, John unconsciously paused for an instant to get his balance. As he did so a scarcely audible sound of light but rapid footfalls greeted his ears, and the same moment there came into view the erect and muscular figure of the Seneca.

The Indian was hardly more than five yards distant. Even in the thick mist and semi-darkness he must have seen John immediately had he paused or so much as turned his head for an instant. Fortunately he did neither and in another second he was out of sight.

"The lead mine!" Jerome whispered, and immediately his imagination pictured some hidden cavern near, and the Indian in the midst of the treasure.

Intent on following the redskin, if possible, the foolhardy boy did not stop to reason or reflect. After Lone-Elk he went and with such speed that soon the savage was only a few paces before him. The Indian halted for a moment. Again brought to the use of his sounder judgment with a jerk, John Jerome stopped no less quickly. Whether some sound, or the prompting of some other of his keen senses had caused the Seneca to pause, the white boy could not determine. But when the Indian moved on, changing his course and heading more directly toward the river, the lad thought twice before he followed.

Could it be that Lone-Elk, well aware that he was being trailed, was only leading his pursuer on, suddenly to turn and kill him when the time and place were to his liking? The thought made John quite uncomfortable.

Then, boy-like, he thought of the lead mine again, thereby deliberately putting temptation before himself; and the next moment he was again in pursuit of the Indian. He heard the fellow now and then, some distance in advance, but did not catch sight of him. It was quite dark now. He must be careful or he would come quite up to the savage without discovering him.

Continuing cautiously, John had traversed nearly a quarter of a mile when he noticed that he no longer heard any sound of the Indian's movements. In vain he listened. The dark, mist-soaked forest was still as death. How in the world could the slippery redskin have disappeared so suddenly?

Afraid to go on lest he fall fairly into the Seneca's arms, hesitating to turn back, the mystified boy stood pondering.

"There's nothing for it but to make a note of this place and come again by daylight. The mine may be very near here," John told himself at last. "It might be all right to wait and see if I don't see a light, after awhile. I most likely would see one if the mine is close by; but it's getting so dark now, and —"

And John Jerome was lost. He looked about, as he reached the conclusion that he must return to his tree, but it was only to realize that he knew not which way to go. How careless he had been! Why had he not observed more carefully the turnings of the chase he had been led? The darkness was deepening fast. He could not see the trees which but a brief time since were distinctly visible.

"Of all the scatter-brain idiots that ever followed a wagon off, I'm the worst, — I am for sure!" the anxious lad told himself, but with quiet determination set about to retrace his steps as best he could.

Not a dozen steps had John taken, however, when he came in contact with a mass of low tangled underbrush. It had not obstructed the way before. Plainly then, he was headed in the wrong direction. Turning, he groped his way first to the right, then to the left. It was all to no purpose; for not one familiar object could he discover, not one thing could he find which would help him to get his bearings.

To be confused and uncertain which way to go in the darkness in one's own home is a most unpleasant predicament. North seems south and right seems left.

On a larger scale and with the calculating part of the situation entirely removed, it was just such a predicament as this in which John was forced at last to acknowledge himself. Worn out, and filled with disappointment and the increasing despair which came with his every attempt to find the direction in which he wished to go, the lad sat down at the foot of a large tree to think. If he could but rid himself of the bewilderment that made him unable even to study out the probability as to which way was which, he would fare much better, he was sure. But the more he tried, the more uncertain he became.

The ground was cold and very wet. The coarse bark of the tree, against which his hand was placed, was moist and clammy to the touch. From the branches above, drops of water came dripping at intervals making what seemed a loud noise as they fell upon the leaves. The security and comparative comforts of the old whitewood seemed very pleasant indeed, now that they were so far from reach, and more than once John wished he had not left them. If the mist would but clear away and the clouds break enough to let him see the stars, he would be able to find his way. Until then, he concluded at last, he would do well to remain where he was.

For a long time. John had remained close to the tree at whose base he had first sat down. Sometimes sitting, sometimes standing, always listening and watching, he believed he had spent the larger part of the long night, when he heard at no great distance the sounds of an axe. Instantly his attention was centered on the noise. It came from the right, the direction in which he felt the hollow poplar to be, though he knew, from trying, that his impression was wrong.

Who could be using an axe in the depths of the forest at midnight? There could be but one answer to the question—the men at the camp in the gully or Lone-Elk.

Thoroughly aroused, John vowed he would learn more. He would see, if he could, what the noise meant. Visions of the lead mine came to him, too, and without more ado he began to feel his way among the trees and through the darkness in the direction from which the sounds reached him. But in scarcely more than a minute the chopping ceased. From the first it had not been loud, sounding rather as if only small bits of wood were being broken up. Now the same awful quiet as before pervaded all the woods.

Only a little way did John venture to go, with nothing to serve as a guide. Very recent experience had taught him the uselessness of trying. But as he stood still, listening for some further sound, he became aware of a certain brightness in the mist some distance off. He guessed at once its meaning. "They were cutting wood to kindle a fire, of course," he told himself. "Now, then, my hunkies, we'll see who you are, at any rate!"

Slowly and with much care to move quietly, John drew nearer the light. Very dull at first, it brightened not a great deal as he approached, so thick was the mist, and indeed it was not until the lad was at the very brink of the bluff above the little gully that he was sure of the location of the fire. As he had supposed, however, the abandoned camp was now occupied. A kettle was hung upon a rude tripod and the cheery blaze was mounting up above it on all sides.

Nothing but the fire and the kettle above it could John see, however, and if anyone was about he was hidden by the fog. No sound reached the watching boy either. Surely, he thought, there was something mysterious here, which hinted of dark secrets and of crime. "But that kettle will boil dry if no one touches it; I'll see something if I wait long enough," John reflected, and he was not kept a great while in suspense.

A tall, uncouth figure of a man dressed in ragged coat and trousers, and wearing a shapeless slouch hat, all of which contrasted oddly with the moccasins on his feet, stepped suddenly from the outer darkness close to the blaze and stooped down, holding his arms about the fire as if he would hug it to him. He shivered and shook himself, then lifted the lid and peeped into the kettle. Sniffing, and nodding his head as though the kettle's contents pleased him, he returned the cover to the pot, then arose and in another second the mist and darkness had swallowed him up again.

To say that John Jerome was greatly interested in what he saw would not be telling the whole truth; for the fact was that he was not only interested, but excited beyond measure. His heart beat fast, and so strongly was he tempted to call out to the fellow that he thought he must hurry away, lest he yield to the strange desire with results which would almost certainly be unfortunate.

There was no doubt in John's mind that here was the murderer of the two men found dead at the "lick." He looked the part, seemed to have "murder" stamped in every fold of his tattered clothing, and on each separate hair of his stubby beard. Even without the evidence which Ree's discovery of the glove had furnished, Jerome would have been certain, he declared within himself, that this man was a vile wretch at best, and capable of committing murder, even if he never had done so. Why was he here? Why did he hide in so secret a place and come out like a fugitive criminal at night to kindle his fire and prepare his food? Where did he stay by day?

These and many more questions came to John as he watched and waited. He wondered, too, whether the fellow was alone. It must be so. He would hear voices otherwise. However, if there were others present he probably would see them soon. They, also, would draw near the fire.

Again the mysterious man came into the firelight. John had a better view of his face this time, but the stubby beard and the long, coarse hair which fell about the fellow's ears concealed his countenance from scrutiny. As before, the man looked into the steaming kettle. Then he rolled a small log nearer to the blaze with his foot and sat down upon it. Presently he lifted the pot from the fire and placed it beside him, as if to cool.

"Ready for you, Lone-Elk, my boy," the fellow called quietly, and in answer to his hoarse voice the outcast Seneca stepped into the circle of

116

light. As if perfectly at home, he, too, seated himself upon the log, and together the repulsive pair began to eat: The white man cut the meat in the kettle with a heavy hunting knife and, using their knives as spears, the two fished out pieces of the boiled leg of venison, for such it appeared to be, and ate greedily.

The sight of Lone-Elk caused John much more alarm than he had yet felt. In a direct line the Indian was but eight or nine yards distant. Fortunately his back was turned, and yet the slightest sound would reach him. Scarcely daring to move, therefore, the lad who watched the strange feast of the redskin and the scarcely less savage-appearing white man, continued a silent spectator of their repast. But when Lone-Elk rose, as if he cared for nothing more, and the white man also got up from the log, as if to say good-bye, John waited no longer. Cautiously as he could, he crept away, lest before he could do so, the Seneca might be up the steep slope and fairly upon him.

CHAPTER XVII – THE EXPLOSION

Thoughts of Simon Girty and of other renegade white men, cut-throats and robbers who had affiliated themselves with hostile Indians, and become more wicked, more merciless, more treacherous than the savages themselves, came to John's mind as he made what haste he could away from the haunted ravine. His reflections did not increase his mental comfort. Far from it; for now he was more anxious than ever for the coming of daylight, or at least a clearing of the weather which would enable him to find security while he pondered on what must be done.

Fearing to go too far lest he again lose himself in the fog, John sat down upon a little log, over which he had partially stumbled, to await the morning. He had listened as best he could but had heard no sound of the Seneca leaving the camp. He thought he had, perhaps, made more haste to get away than was really necessary, after all, and as his excitement cooled, he was tempted again to take a peep at the strange scene he had witnessed. This notion, however, the lad put steadily behind him. He would not be too venturesome, he told himself. Even as it was he would get a good-natured scolding from Kingdom for having left the old poplar.

The light in the distance, dimly visible through the mist, slowly faded. The campfire was dying out. Lone-Elk was gone now, no doubt, but which direction had he taken? John hoped he would not go to the clearing and by hanging about there keep Kingdom from setting forth. It would be remarkable if the Seneca could find his way. Moreover, Ree would be leaving the cabin before daylight. Maybe he had started even now.

The dawn came just when John bad ceased to look for and momentarily expect it. Indeed, he was quite surprised to notice suddenly that objects near were again visible. He made out nothing clearly, but he could see a few feet in each direction and it was enough. Without hesitation, and almost without stopping to note the way he was taking, he headed instinctively toward the old poplar and without the least trouble reached its shelter not many minutes later.

His nerves still at high tension after the night's experience, Jerome's efforts to catch a wink of sleep were quite unavailing. He fell to thinking of the probable results which would have followed his shooting Lone-Elk as the Indian sat beside the campfire. He thought more of the secret lead mine and wondered if the villainous appearing white man and the Seneca were not partners in that enterprise. Surely there was reason to believe such to be the case. What other explanation of the white man's companionship with the Indian could be presented?

At last, when the daylight had fully come, John fell asleep. He was still dreaming when Ree Kingdom came and the latter, little guessing that he had not been sleeping just as soundly the whole night through, roused him with:

"I declare, old chap, you seem to find this old tree as comfortable as a feather bed!"

"Guess you would, too, Ree, if you'd been watching midnight feasts, and didn't know but they were cannibal feasts at that, and had been kept up all night."

With a grin John noticed the surprise his words caused, and a determination he had formed earlier to break the news of his discoveries gently was forgotten. In another minute he had related the substance of his night's adventure.

"Well, say! I think you did have a busy night!" Ree exclaimed. "We've found the mine, John! There's no two ways about that! If that lead mine is not within a mighty short distance of the camp of those fellows, then I'm no prophet!"

Kingdom's interest and pleasure in the discovery John had made could scarcely have been greater. But putting the subject aside for the moment, he gave his companion all the interesting information obtained from Fishing Bird, and the two then set about to plan their next movements. Quite naturally both wished to pay another visit to the strange camp in the gully.

To do so, however, involved much risk. Lone-Elk might be, in fact, probably was, still loitering near. Again, if the occupant or occupants of the camp discovered that their presence was known to other white men, they would be very likely to change their location, and, no doubt, do all in their power to conceal every evidence of the lead mine's existence.

"We've got to come upon them by surprise and not only capture the murderers of the men at the salt springs, but find the mine at the same time," said John.

"If the mine is there, which we don't know, but only believe," Ree made answer. "Still," he went on, "there's only one other way to do it, and that is to keep a watch on the camp all the time till we find out more about it. Lone-Elk,—bless him!—is in the way of that program. And there's another thing to think about, which is, what are we going to do with the murderers when we capture them!"

"Well, we can hardly say,'Come along now, and be hanged, as you deserve,'" Jerome suggested.

For some time Kingdom was silent. At last he said, very thoughtfully and slowly:

"John, you must go to Fort Pitt or to Wayne's army. You must tell whoever is in charge just what has been found at the 'lick' and in the woods here. Bring back four or five good men and we'll seize the camp down there and everything and everybody in it. The men you bring can take the murderers back for trial, and I only hope we can find some evidence that will send the Seneca along with them."

"But if we do, we may as well pull up stakes and go along ourselves, Ree. The Delawares would say we had been acting as spies for Wayne, sure!"

"We can tell what to do about that when the time comes," was the answer. "We know now that it won't do for us to attack the camp alone. We'd have a whole pack of warriors down on us before we could get a day's march away. We know that a murder has been committed and I hope we know what our solemn duty is, even if the finding of the lead mine be left out of consideration altogether."

"Wouldn't you rather find the mine without letting everybody else know about it? I would," John argued. "Not but what I like your plan all right," he added, "but if Wayne's army gets to find out there is a lead mine, and finds out where it is, too, I don't see how the fact that we know of it, the same as Lone-Elk, is going to do us any good with King Pipe."

This reasoning puzzled Kingdom. In one way John was right, and he was forced to admit it. But he argued that, as law-abiding citizens, it was their duty to expose the murder that had been committed; that if they did not do so, they were parties to the crime, the more particularly so since they held in their possession evidence so positive against the slayers of the two men at the springs.

"I don't see why we need tell Wayne about the mine at all. It hasn't anything to do with the case anyway," Jerome made answer.

"All right. For we know of the one thing, and the mine is just our supposition, after all," was Ree's decision. "What we should or shouldn't tell we shall know when the time comes. You start for Pittsburg today, and I'll manage somehow to keep yonder robbers' roost under my eye till you are back with some reliable men. And I tell you, John, don't bring green militia men, but good fighters — men who know the woods."

"I feel it in my bones, Ree, that this is going to be the end of the log house on the Cuyahoga," John remarked somewhat later. "Mind you, I'm not scared, and I'm not particularly caring if such a thing does happen, but the time has come when we've got to be either with the Indians or against them. Sure as the world, the Delawares will go against us for good, if we bring Wayne's men here."

"Maybe so; but we can only do what we think is the right thing to be done. Then we can face Captain Pipe or anybody else with a clean conscience.

Don't be so glum, though! We've come through trouble far worse than this, and with flying colors!"

It may have been that John Jerome received for a moment a glimpse of the future which Kingdom did not have. The latter took a cheerful view of the outcome of their plans. John could not do so, though usually optimistic. He did not hang back, however, nor question further the wisdom of his companion's desire to put into the hands of the law the fact that two apparently peaceable salt boilers had been most wickedly slain.

Kingdom had brought to the hollow whitewood a generous supply of provisions, also fresh powder, lest John's stock had become damp and useless from the wet weather of the day before. There was no reason, then, why Jerome should not start at once with his message to Wayne, or to Fort Pitt, if "Mad Anthony" should be found no longer in his camp lower down on the Ohio. Thus, soon after a definite decision was reached by the boys, the younger lad set out.

It was left to John to choose his own time and course, but he told Ree he would aim to strike the direct trail to Fort Pitt about a day's journey eastward from the cabin. With care, he hoped to avoid all possibly hostile Indians, and he would reach the Ohio in less than a week. Wayne's men would wish, no doubt, to visit the salt springs to see the bodies of the murdered men before undertaking to apprehend the murderers, and so nearly two weeks must elapse before he would see Kingdom again. The latter agreed to be waiting for him, no matter when he came, and was hopeful he would have good news of some kind to impart by that time. Encouraged thus, and more cheerful than he had been for a time, John began his long journey just as the shadows indicated the hour of noon.

A south breeze and the sun had scattered the mist and the weather gave promise of being fine and warm for many days to come. John felt the influence of nature's brighter aspect at once when fairly under way, and would have looked upon his journey as upon a pleasant holiday had he had Kingdom's company. But that was not to be and he could only resolve to cover as much ground as possible every day. As he thought of the object of his journey, too, his interest in it increased and he anticipated with much satisfaction his pride in guiding a small company of soldiers through the woods on the important mission, for which, he was sure, Gen. Wayne would at once cause men to be detailed.

Anxious to avoid a possible meeting with Lone-Elk, the young woodsman traveled with much caution, especially this first day. Later, when he had left the cabin far behind, he made less effort to conceal his trail and ceased to watch as vigilantly as before. To an accident, as much as to any recklessness on his part, however, was due the sudden ending of John's expectations.

The boy had been three days upon the well-marked trail leading to the Ohio river and thence along that stream to Fort Pitt. It was the evening of his fourth day since parting from Kingdom. He kindled a small fire close beside a large rock, thinking to have some warm meat for supper, then go on a half mile or more and sleep wherever chance offered. He would thus be well away from the scene by the time his fire attracted attention, if attract attention it should.

John had placed his blanket and other surplus baggage upon the big rock and walked some distance away to gather fine, dry wood. Suddenly a terrific explosion occurred. The young traveler saw his fire go flying in all directions, while a perfect shower of leaves, small sticks and bits of earth was dashed likewise into the air. He knew instantly what had happened. The extra pouch of powder Ree had brought for him had rolled from the big stone directly into the blaze.

There was only one thing to do and that must be done quickly. The tremendous noise of the explosion would be heard for a long distance. So much louder than the report of a rifle was it that if Indians or others were within hearing they would most certainly make immediate investigation. Without losing a moment, therefore, John seized his blanket and other baggage which had been jarred off the stone, but away from the fire, fortunately, and rushed away through the woods at high speed.

Now, anyone coming up to the place, drawn thither by the great noise, would be most likely to come by way of the trail, from one direction or the other, John Jerome quite properly reasoned so, leaving the path at a sharp angle, he struck through the forest to the north.

Fortune plays strange tricks with all of us. The whimsical dame played one on John which he long remembered; for as he ran on and on among the trees, dodging in and out among the bushes in the dim twilight, he almost collided with a party of Indians hurrying almost as fast in one direction as he was fleeing in the other.

CHAPTER XVIII — FISHING BIRD IN TROUBLE

The days were always long to Kingdom when John was gone. From their childhood they had been much together. Even in the time of his bound-boy experience, with a harsh master to serve, Ree had found time for play occasionally only because John helped him with his work. He had never known any other intimate companion; had never cared for any. Now, far from all other friends, he valued John Jerome's friendship all the more and counted the days until the cheerful, helpful lad would be returning.

Yet Kingdom had much to do even while he watched and waited. Lone-Elk frequently hovered near. He had grown more sullen and ugly than at first and Ree had little doubt of the fate the cabin would suffer if the Indian were but given a chance to act without danger that he would be discovered. To watch for the Seneca's coming, then, and to keep an eye on him while he flitted about the edge of the clearing, disappearing, reappearing, coming and going like the ominous shadow he was, became as much a daily task as the care of the two horses.

Twice in a week's time Ree found opportunities to visit the vicinity of the mysterious camp in the gully. He saw no one, but he never remained long, for the freshness of the ashes and the altered position of the log in front of them each time were assurance that the tenants were not far away.

It was the lead mine which kept the camp occupied, Kingdom now was certain. The hidden treasure could not be far away. He had no doubt of his ability to find it if but given the chance to make unmolested search.

It was while on little hunting trips into the woods to the north that the boy had visited the strange camping place. Though he made it a rule never to go a great distance from the cabin, game was plentiful and he rarely, if ever, returned empty-handed. The season for hunting and trapping was now at its beginning. Each taste of its pleasures made the young pioneer long for the end of the trouble with Lone-Elk and a return of the days of security and care-free happiness which both he and John had so much enjoyed in the past. The thought that they would not return — not, at least, until after many days and many dangers that he little anticipated, — did not so much as come to his confident, self-reliant brain.

Not since the "talk" with the Delawares had Kingdom been near Captain Pipe's village. He seldom left the clearing to go even a little distance in that direction, though often he wished he might do so; often wished he could talk the whole trouble over with Captain Pipe alone; often wished Fishing Bird would come, even if he brought no news. The friendly Delaware, he felt certain, feared for his own safety every time he visited the clearing. He must have given up his watching of the Seneca, too. Perhaps he had been warned to do so. Time would tell.

Thinking of these things, thinking of John, thinking of the work before him, Kingdom was busily occupied one afternoon, tying choice ears of corn together by the husks to hang them from the roof poles, when rapid footsteps near the open door caused him to spring hastily up.

"Hello, here! Howdy, little brothers!" he exclaimed heartily, for before him stood Little Wolf and Long-Hair, two Indian boys, both of whom had shown for the young white settlers a warm friendship.

With the true Indian showing of unmoved indifference, the Delaware lads returned the greeting and Kingdom at once led them into the cabin and set before them the choicest bits of meat and bread the larder afforded.

As the youthful braves ate, Ree inquired kindly concerning Captain Pipe, Neohaw and others of the Delawares, and presently asked about Fishing Bird — desired to know if the spirits prospered him and where he had been so long that his Paleface friends had seen nothing of him.

Ree did not recall the fact at the moment, but he remembered a few seconds later that Long-Hair was a brother of Fishing Bird, — a relationship which soon explained the object of the visit of the Indian lads.

"Fishing Bird — him Long-Hair and Little Wolf come to tell White Fox about," the former said. "Fishing Bird was hunting. Long-Knives caught him and Long-Knives going to kill Fishing Bird dead."

"Long-Hair! What are you saying? What do you mean!" cried Kingdom with such solemn but keen earnestness that the Delaware boy was quite startled. "Who will harm Fishing Bird?"

"Yep; just as Long-Hair says," put in Little Wolf. "Palefaces made Fishing Bird prisoner, where Paleface army is at the River Ohio, and going to kill him."

"Tell me, brothers, how do you know this? Were you sent to tell the White Fox?" asked Ree, calling himself by the name the Indians had long ago given him. "This is terrible news you bring me! It cannot be!"

Both the little redskins slowly nodded their heads in solemn confirmation of all they had said.

"From Fort Pitt a runner came, telling Hopocon how Fishing Bird a prisoner is—made a prisoner by Captain Wayne's warriors," said Long-Hair with the air of being a full-fledged warrior himself. "Gentle Maiden said Long-Hair must come fast and tell White Fox."

"Little Wolf come too," said the other youngster, bound to be included.

"You both did just right. Gentle Maiden did right also; for White Fox will not for a great deal let harm come to Fishing Bird, if he can help it," Kingdom briskly replied. "White Fox is going right away to 'Captain' Wayne's men. Little Brothers will go back and tell Gentle Maiden this. Tell Gentle Maiden, and any others who ask, that Fishing Bird shall be set free if White Fox and Little Paleface can possibly do it."

Even as he spoke, Ree's mind was made up. In fifteen minutes he had saddled Phoebe, turned Neb out to graze and was closing the cabin preparatory to a rapid ride to Wayne's encampment. The Indian boys watched him gallop across the clearing, his rifle hanging before him from the saddle, his powder horn and bullet pouch, both freshly refilled, slung from his shoulder, his blanket and a hastily collected supply of provisions taking the usual place of saddle bags.

"White Fox is a mighty warrior," said Little Wolf admiringly.

"White Fox is too good to be a Paleface. Fishing Bird says the same thing," Long-Hair made answer.

But Lone-Elk and a white man who was with him, crouching in the bushes by the river, watched the young horseman speed into the woods with altogether different feelings.

Fishing Bird had been a prisoner in the strong, log guard-house more than four days at the time Kingdom dashed away to his rescue. The friendly Delaware, together with three others, had made the journey to the Ohio, drawn thither by curiosity, and perhaps, too, with some expectation of gaining intelligence of the increasing strength of the white commander's forces.

Friendly Indians were coming and going in the vicinity of Wayne's "Legion" constantly, and the Delawares undoubtedly counted upon being classed among the neutral savages. But "Mad Anthony" was not asleep. While he waited to receive new recruits from the east, and drill his men to a point of proper efficiency, before making a start into hostile Indian country, he was constantly informing himself of the doings of the redskins in the interior—in the northwest country, where, he knew, the inevitable battle would eventually be.

Wayne's staff of loyal scouts and trained woodsmen were likewise alert. Every day they gathered from one source or another some news of the preparations all the northwest tribes were making for a fight, which, they told one another, would sicken the Palefaces more than the defeat of St. Clair had done, and check the advance of the settlers upon their forest lands forever.

Unfortunately for Fishing Bird, it so happened that, just at the time he and his friends were spying about in the vicinity of the white army, Gen. Wayne ordered that some Indian from the interior be brought in and questioned. Six men went out to find and capture such a redskin.

128

They came upon the little party of Delawares, encamped several miles from the river, just at daybreak. All were sleeping, but they heard the white men stealing upon them, and dashed into the woods without firing a shot. Three made their escape. One was caught and the unhappy Fishing Bird was he.

Matters were made worse for the captive, too, by the redskins who had eluded capture returning and firing upon the white scouts. They intended, no doubt, to assist Fishing Bird to get away. But they caused him only so much the more trouble; for his captors made him bear the brunt of the wrath the hostile act excited in their minds. The still further result was that Fishing Bird, being mistreated, became ugly and obstinate. He refused to talk. He would tell the Palefaces nothing. Let them beat him, abuse and torture him as they would, he bore it all in sullen, defiant silence.

"Chuck him in the guard-house! Starve him! Let him know that he's got to talk or die! Hang all the rascals, anyhow!" a captain had exclaimed, and the unoffending Delaware was hustled off in no very tender manner.

Gen. Wayne soon learned of what had taken place and caused Fishing Bird to be brought to his own cabin. He talked kindly to the Indian, but the latter was still smarting physically from the injuries, and smarting still more mentally from the bitter injustice of the punishment he had received, and remained obstinate.

"He evidently knows something. If he had nothing to tell he would be talkative enough," "Mad Anthony" thought, and ordered Fishing Bird taken back to the guard-house. "Let him understand that he will not be harmed if he'll tell the truth," he said, "but if he won't talk — "

In a short time the peaceable redskins in the vicinity learned what had been done with the Delaware and so before a great while the information reached the three warriors who had been his companions. Immediately they carried word to Captain Pipe. The latter was too proud to call upon Return Kingdom to exert himself in Fishing Bird's behalf, after the manner in which he had allowed the white boy to be treated, but Gentle Maiden did not hesitate. She sent Long-Hair and Little Wolf to the cabin at once.

None of the Indians really knew, however, the many reasons Kingdom had for showing his friendship for Fishing Bird in the latter's hour of need. They may have known that the two were more than usually friendly, but they did not guess how the young white settlers had often been assisted by the Delaware; nor did anyone besides Ree and John and Fishing Bird himself know of the terrible struggle in the woods that night two years ago, when Kingdom was so near to killing the young savage.

The circumstances of the capture and detention of Fishing Bird were not, of course, known to Kingdom until he reached Wayne's camp. Indeed, he puzzled his mind a great deal with the subject, as he traveled rapidly along the old trail to the east. Sometimes at a gallop, sometimes at a walk, he kept to the course, but wherever the path would permit of it, he let Phoebe take her fastest gait and urged the docile and only too willing mare on and on.

Ree camped at evening beneath some heavy, overhanging bushes at the foot of a steep hill. The night passed without incident and was followed by a long, hard day in the saddle. Every minute seemed most precious to the anxious boy and every delay of any kind vexed and worried him. He feared constantly that he would reach his destination too late. The very thought that he would arrive only to learn that the good, loyal Fishing Bird had been put to death filled him with anguish and alarm.

Hardly could Kingdom endure to spend another night in camp. He wished to be pushing forward. The delay of many hours was more than irksome. But he could make little progress in the darkness, he knew, and Phoebe would be the better the next day for the rest. Luckily the weather remained pleasant. Fortune favored him in this respect, at least. The second night of his journey, therefore, Ree spent in a sheltered spot beside a little stream, where a fine growth of grass afforded his horse abundant feed.

Twice in the hour of darkness the lad heard far off an Indian's war-whoop. The sound alarmed him a great deal; not for his own safety so much as for the reason it gave him for believing the trouble along the border was far worse than he had supposed. And such, in fact, was the case, as the youthful pioneer was soon to learn.

For the time, however, the threatening, distant cries served only to make the solitary traveler somewhat uneasy in his lonely camp. But with the coming of morning, he thought little more of the matter, and it was not until he reached Wayne's outposts and found that John Jerome had not arrived there that the night's disturbing sounds caused him any further anxiety.

CHAPTER XIX — AN INTERVIEW WITH "MAD ANTHONY"

The satisfaction and pleasure Kingdom felt in finding that Fishing Bird, though a prisoner, was still unharmed, was mixed with much distress by the knowledge that nothing had been seen of John Jerome at Wayne's camp. True, it might be that John had gone directly to Fort Pitt; but even in doing so he would pass in the immediate vicinity of the military encampment and it would be strange if he did not stop.

Not the least light could any of the scouts or others with whom Ree talked throw upon the mystery of the missing boy. They agreed with his friend that he should have arrived at the Ohio several days ago, at least. Their views of the whole matter were most discouraging. Kingdom did not realize, they insisted, that the woods were full of hostile Indian bands; that all up and down the Ohio and for many miles in all directions, there was burning, pillaging and murder almost every day, and no man was safe when alone.

Neither did Kingdom receive the least encouragement when he suggested that a rescue party be formed to search for his missing chum. Gen. Wayne would not think of it, the men said. It was no unusual thing for a man to be taken prisoner, no unusual thing for a lone hunter to be scalped. If the army were to undertake the rescue of every captive, or the punishment of every party of Indian marauders, there would be time for nothing else.

"Still, I must see Gen. Wayne himself," Kingdom insisted. "Even if I can do nothing else for John Jerome, perhaps I can obtain freedom for Fishing Bird, and he and I can do something."

Still the party of petty officers, scouts, and soldiers with whom Kingdom talked shook their heads, and it was only after considerable urging that one of the men said he would try to arrange matters for Ree to see the commander.

Kingdom had reached the encampment of Wayne's "Legion" at about mid-day. It was late in the afternoon when his new-found friend, a sergeant named Quayle, consented to see if Ree could not have a talk with Gen. Wayne himself. The delay seemed past all understanding to Kingdom, little acquainted with army customs and discipline. And when the sergeant returned, bringing a superior officer with him, who, after talking with the anxious lad, told him that the general would see him in the morning, Kingdom's patience was sorely tried indeed. He did, however, obtain an assurance from the officer that Fishing Bird would be well treated and injured no further until he could present his petition for the Indian's release, and with this he endeavored to be content.

Unwilling to tell his whole story to anyone but "Mad Anthony" himself, Kingdom was unable to give the men with whom he mingled a great deal of information. They plied him with countless questions concerning the movements and general attitude of the Indians of the interior, and his experiences with them, but the heart-sick boy felt little disposed to talk and gave them no more than civil answers. In vain he tried to get permission to visit Fishing Bird in the guard-house. Serg. Quayle told him it would be of no use, but not until one higher in authority had kindly but very definitely refused did Ree give up.

Every hope Kingdom ventured to entertain now centered in Gen. Wayne, and time and again he went over in his mind all that he meant to say to the commander when the time came.

He saw to it that Phoebe was given a place among the horses in the camp and properly fed and cared for, then accepted an invitation extended by his friend, the sergeant, to have supper and spend the night with him.

Had his thoughts been less occupied with the strange disappearance of John, and with his anxiety concerning the outcome of his interview with Gen. Wayne, Ree would have spent a jolly evening among the care-free spirits,—woodsmen, adventurers, regular soldiers and raw recruits who made up the bulk of the "Legion."

There was romance in the life of nearly every man about him. There were stories untold, but to some extent readable, in the faces and figures and ways of all the scouts, the hardened Indian fighters, and the seasoned soldiers. There was much of interest, too, among the great variety of fellows who were plainly not long from the east. Some were outcasts and downright criminals undoubtedly; some were sons of highly respected fathers, banished from home, perhaps, or here only in search of adventure and excitement. Their stories, their songs, their speech and their dress all told of the strangely different walks of life from which they had come; and gathered together here on the border of the great wilderness, while the campfires brightly burned, they made a truly romantic picture.

It was a picture which would live in history, too, as time in due course told; for in the end it proved that no more efficient force ever invaded hostile Indian territory than Wayne led to final victory over the savages who had vowed to make the Ohio river the boundary between themselves and civilization for all time.

The-men with whom Ree came in contact were, in their rough way, very kind to the young man from the depths of the woods. They urged him to join them and go down the Ohio and thence march into the woods with them, and they assured him that he would never find a better chief than "Old Mad Anthony." To all these proposals Kingdom answered that he could think of nothing of the kind until John Jerome was found, living or dead, for which sentiment Sergeant Quayle heartily commended him.

For the most part the men of Wayne's command slept in the open air, but Sergeant Quayle and his intimate associates had erected a shelter of bark laid up against a pole placed across two forked sticks. Although one side of this crude structure was entirely open to the weather, the campfire made the fact scarcely unpleasant, and Kingdom found the soldiers' quarters quite comfortable. The lad was astir by the time the first early risers of the army were moving about, however, and impatiently waited the coming of the aide who was to lake him to Gen. Wayne's quarters.

At last came the lieutenant whom Ree had seen the day before. With scarcely a word he signaled with a nod to the lad to accompany him, and

134

silently conducted the young frontiersman to a substantial log house. With a word to a sentry near, the officer opened the door and motioned to Kingdom to enter.

"Mad Anthony" sat at breakfast alone. He looked up with sharp but not unkind scrutiny of his visitor as, cap in hand, the boy softly closed the door and stood awaiting his notice.

"Sit down there and tell me your story," said the commander rather brusquely, indicating a three-legged stool near his table. Although he spoke in a quick, decisive way his voice was the kind which inspires confidence and the young visitor, though somewhat nervous, at no time was disconcerted by the business-like manner of the great soldier.

"Gladly, sir," said Kingdom, seating himself, but for a moment hesitating just where to begin.

"Well, well, proceed then!" the general urged with a smile, and without further loss of time the boy told briefly who he was and what had brought him to the soldiers' camp. He mentioned John Jerome's connection with his story and John's disappearance, alluding only briefly, for the time, to the murder at the salt springs, and to the charge of witchcraft that had been the beginning of the trouble. Of the lead mine he did not speak.

"I see no reason why we cannot give this Indian you are interested in his liberty," said the general, when Ree had concluded. "But I am much afraid we can do nothing for your friend. Very likely he will turn up safe and sound before long. I am bound to say, though, that my advice to you would be that you do not go back to your cabin until these troublous times are over. How would you like to come with my men — be one of my scouts and interpreters? Come, now?"

Poor Ree, sadly disheartened, could only reply that if circumstances were different he would very much like to do so; but as it was, well, he simply couldn't do anything until John Jerome was found. Then he told more fully of the trouble with Lone-Elk and how it had happened to result in the discovery of the two murdered men at the big "lick."

Made more confident by Gen. Wayne's interest, he told of the strange camp in the gully and his reason for believing that the salt springs murderer or murderers were there.

"You may be right," said the commander, "and you may be wrong. That two men, — apparently men not fully accustomed to the woods, — should have been killed and their bodies concealed in the brush, is, in these times, not surprising. And the fact being that these men are to us unknown, while it does not make the murder less distressing or less a crime, does present a reason for our not being duty bound to unravel the mystery and attempt to punish the perpetrators of the deed. In short, if we begin to follow up singly each red-handed outrage committed along the border, we shall not have men for anything else. We can only bide our time and strike the savages collectively — strike a blow that will bring both them and their British supporters to their senses — a blow with something of suddenness about it."

Kingdom's hopes had dwindled to nothing. He wanted help, help to find John Jerome, help to carry out his plan to capture the salt springs criminals, and while he was about it, help to show Lone-Elk that he had powerful friends at his back who might make very costly to the Seneca any injury which was done the two young settlers on the land for which the Delawares had received a fair price.

Of course Gen. Wayne saw the whole trend of Kingdom's thoughts. There is a power possessed, as a rule, by great generals in every walk of life, by which they see at a glance the workings of the minds of the less mature or less able men about them. Kingdom, however, was bright enough to understand all this perfectly, even while "Mad Anthony" talked with him. He felt that an injustice was done him. He knew that his motives were not by any means as selfish as they seemed. But how could he make himself better understood? He hesitated to try, and in his extremity, he played his last card — the lead mine.

Who can blame Return Kingdom if, when he told Gen. Wayne of the Seneca's secret, he went just a little beyond actual facts in his representation of the certainty of the mine's existence! That he had never seen the mine, he was forced, as the commander questioned him, to admit. Yes, it was true, he acknowledged, that he had never heard of the lead mine before Lone-Elk came among the Delawares. Neither had he seen any lead from the mine, nor could he tell positively of any Indian who had seen any. The story Fishing Bird had told was the whole basis of his assertion that there was a lead mine somewhere along the Cuyahoga, and presumably it was not far from the mysterious camp in the ravine.

"Now have I all the information you can give me on this subject?" asked Gen. Wayne, with something of a twinkle in his eye.

"Yes, sir," Kingdom answered, the twinkle somehow making him feel more comfortable than he did before.

"All right, then," and the general stepped to the door. "Have that Indian, Fishing Bird, brought to headquarters," he said to the man outside.

"Mad Anthony" paced thoughtfully up and down the earthen floor of the single room of the cabin while he waited. Wondering, and more hopeful now, Kingdom tried to determine what the commander meant to do by glancing often at his knitted brow.

In five minutes the Delaware, with a sullen air of pride, stepped into the cabin. In an instant, however, his manner changed. A look of pleasure came to his eyes and he held out his hand to Kingdom.

The greeting between the young woodsman and the Indian was pleasant to see. As soon as they had silently shaken hands, however, Gen. Wayne said:

"Now, Fishing Bird, what can you tell me of a lead mine near your Cuyahoga river!"

137

"The lead mine is the secret of Lone-Elk—Lone-Elk, the Seneca," the Delaware made answer.

"Well, if I give you your liberty, will you go with this young man, your friend here, and some men I shall send with you, and see if you can find this mine? And will you help my young friend, whom you seem to know rather better than I do, find the boy who is accused of witchcraft?"

"Anything White Fox asks will Fishing Bird do," the Indian replied, with quiet dignity.

CHAPTER XX – DELIVERED TO THE DELAWARES

The effort it cost John Jerome to conceal his astonishment and his chagrin as he encountered the savages hurrying toward the scene of the explosion, from which he was hastening away, would be hard to describe. But he controlled himself sufficiently to say:

"Hello, here, brothers! Don't go up there or you may get blown sky high! My powder pouch fell into the' fire, and it tore things up to beat the Dutch."

With this greeting and hastily given explanation of his being found running away, the boy was starting on, thinking to be gone before the Indians had recovered from their own surprise; but in this he was disappointed. One fellow seized his hand, as if merely to shake it in friendly salutation, but continued to hold it and would not let him take it away. Quickly the other savages gathered near and, though but a few seconds had passed, John saw that he was a prisoner and that his escape was intentionally cut completely off.

The situation seemed to give the Indians vastly more pleasure than it gave Jerome. Their amusement and delight made itself manifest in curious ways. One, with a great show of interest, took the boy's rifle from him and pretended to examine it as though it were some very rare specimen. Another did likewise with his pistols, while a third bore off his powder horn. Still others playfully rapped their victim's shins and head with their gun barrels, driving him at last to such desperation that when one particularly playful fellow pricked him suddenly from behind with a knife-point, he wheeled and with clenched fist sent the redskin sprawling among the leaves.

The savage retaliated with the butt of his rifle, but now the party started on, two of them leading John between them, and for the time the annoyances ceased. The Indians went at once to the spot where the explosion had occurred, plainly marked in the gathering gloom by the remnants of the campfire. They inspected the locality with considerable interest. There was little to see, however, and in a short time they were under way again. Their course, John was sorry to see, was in the direction of the Delaware village on the lake.

Not until darkness made it quite impossible to go further did the savages pause. They chose as a camping place a slight depression in the ground, among some maples. The wind had gathered a deep drift of autumn leaves here, and as the captive lay down between two of the captors, he found his bed not otherwise uncomfortable. A long piece of untanned buckskin had been tied about his waist, however, and as its loose ends were tied to the waists of the Indians beside him, he realized that escape would be all but impossible.

John had had abundant opportunity to study the Indians while on the march, but the fading light had made it impossible to see them distinctly. There were seven in the party, all young, active fellows, and all strangers. They were Shawnees, John decided. Where they had been, and whither they were going he could not guess. He did know that it would be pleasanter lying between the two redskins who guarded him, if they would but give him more room, and he knew that the paint bedecking the band was no sign of good. Not wholly hopeless, however, he fell asleep at last, wondering what Ree was doing.

With daylight's coming the Indians kindled a fire and broiled some venison. They allowed their prisoner to eat all he wished, nor for the present was he tortured further with such antics as had been indulged in the night before. No haste was made to break camp and be on the move again by the band, but to the contrary, they were very deliberate in all they did. During the morning they held a council and, though they spoke in guarded tones, John knew that he was the subject of their talk.

The captive was glad to believe that none of the Indians knew him. They would be for taking him directly to the Delaware town, to place him at, the mercy of Lone-Elk, if they were aware of the charge against him, he was certain. If the savages asked him anything, he would in self-defense be bound to deceive them. Thinking of this made John think of deceiving the band still further. He would cause the savages to believe that he was from Detroit, a British spy sent to ascertain the extent of Wayne's forces, and, of course, friendly to the Indians.

The boy's opportunity to put his plan into practice came rather sooner than he expected. Within a few minutes one of the redskins who had their heads together in conference, came to him and asked in very fair English who he was and what he was doing in the woods so far from the settlements.

"It's about time you were finding out, I think," John answered, with a show of injured innocence. "At Detroit we are taught to believe that the English and the Indians are brothers. We both hate the Americans, who are robbing all the tribes of the Northwest just as they robbed the Eastern tribes long ago, yet when my chief sends me to find out what moves the Americans are making to march into the forests of the Indians, lo! a party of my red brothers seize me and treat me as a prisoner!"

The savage to whom John addressed his words of well-feigned righteous wrath looked puzzled, then a grin spread itself slowly over his lips. He summoned the other Indians and told them, in substance, what the captive said. Then in a tongue John did not understand he added a few words which made them all smile.

Very much afraid that in some way he had gotten himself into a predicament, with his hastily concocted story, the lad felt at heart that he might have fared as well if he had told the truth; but having made a start upon a different road he was unwilling to turn back.

Even when one of the redskins began to question him as to when he had left Detroit, and with whom and by what route he had traveled, he maintained his air of offended friendship, and answered as best he could. Asked the name of the person in command at Detroit at the time he left, he promptly answered, "Col. John Jenkins, and you ought to know it, if you know anything about Detroit at all."

John used the first name which came to him in replying to this question, and he answered many others just as rashly. From appearing puzzled the savages now seemed mightily amused. The prisoner noted the fact with chagrin, but stuck resolutely to his original story. The climax came, however, when he was asked if there had been much snow at Detroit when he left.

"Why, no; not much to speak of," he promptly answered.

The Indians looked at one another and grinned. Then one of them turned to him.

"Paleface heap big liar," he said.

"Why? Why am I? Because I said that there wasn't much snow? Well there wasn't! Of course there was lots of snow, but it wasn't any seven or eight feet deep!"

"One heap big fool liar," the redskin reiterated.

The Indians seemed to have satisfied themselves completely as to the truthfulness of the prisoner. They gave his words no further attention, and how bitterly crestfallen, and in his heart ashamed and disgraced, he felt, no one knew so well as he, as they turned away to resume their conference.

John realized that he had probably made bad matters worse. Seeing how anxious he was to deceive them, the redskins would be more than ordinarily distrustful of him and perhaps conclude that he was one who, for some reason, was particularly hostile to them. They asked him no more questions now, but appeared to guard him even more closely than before.

John thought so, at least, for his mind was turning with increased attentiveness to the possibility of escape. Not the slightest prospect that a favorable opportunity would come to him did he see, however, and when the Indians resumed their journey a little later, he was put between the two most villainous looking fellows in the band.

The course the savages took, in starting off this time, was slightly different from that pursued the night before. As nearly as John could reckon it would, if continued, land them, at the end of two or three days, at the "Crossing Place of the Muskingum," the point at which the Great Trail from Pittsburg to Detroit crossed the Muskingum river. Where this particular party of savages did eventually find themselves, though, John Jerome never knew, nor did he ever learn definitely that they had come from Detroit, as he suspected.

The reason for this presented itself the second day after the cross-questioning of the prisoner and the wretched failure of his effort to deceive. The Indians encamped at noon, after a leisurely journey through a fine forest country, beside a little spring bubbling from under the very trunk of a mammoth oak. They lingered here several hours and while they waited a party of five bucks from Captain Pipe's town chanced suddenly upon them.

John recognized the fellows immediately. He knew, too, that they recognized him, though they did not at once pay any attention to him. It was not until after quite extensive greetings between them and the seven warriors in the Shawnee party, in fact, that they bestowed even a look upon the prisoner. Then they turned toward him with grins of malicious pleasure.

Having learned that their prisoner was none other than the "witch," of whom they had heard as having been the cause of the death of that well known warrior, Big Buffalo, the Shawnees plainly regarded him now as a dangerous individual. A little later he was the subject of a long conversation between the young Delawares and his captors and the wretched boy quickly discovered that his worst fears were realized. For the five from Pipe's town were anxious to have him taken to their village, and the Shawnees appeared not to object.

At some length the Delawares told of the certain evidence Lone-Elk had discovered — the hatchet found in the corn — the very hatchet with which

143

Big Buffalo was killed, and of the long and fruitless search that had been made for the "witch." They urged the Shawnees to come and see the Paleface burned, and the killing of one of the greatest warriors of the Delawares avenged.

In turn the band into whose merciless hands poor John had fallen told of the exciting times along the border, of burning and killing both by night and by day. They told, too, of much powder and much lead which the Indians could obtain at Detroit, and two of them exhibited brand new rifles. While they were anxious to see the "witch" destroyed, they said, they did not wish to go to Pipe's town as they were on their way to a fruitful source of plunder.

As John heard and understood a considerable part of the conversation, a determination to escape or die in the attempt rapidly grew within him. And when he heard an agreement reached that he should be turned over to the Delawares, while the Shawnees continued on their way, he set his mind intently upon the problem of getting away, or making an effort at least, let the cost be what it might.

The Shawnees turned John over to the Delawares, after binding him securely, with many a kick and cuff. They particularly denounced him as a "forked-tongued witch," and worked themselves into such passions of hatred that the prisoner was in imminent danger of being killed then and there.

With his hands tied behind him, and led and dragged by a long rope of rawhide about his neck, the captive was taken in charge by the Delawares, and the two Indian bands set off in different directions. The mission of the Shawnees, as has been stated, John never learned; but he well knew the destination of the five young Delawares, and a lump of pain and bitterness grew big in his throat as he thought of the cowardice and wretched injustice of it all.

CHAPTER XXI — THE BURNING OF THE CABIN

Indian troubles along the border were perhaps never worse in the history of the Northwest territory than in this year (1792) when Return Kingdom and John Jerome daily lived surrounded by dangers, the true, awful extent of which they little realized.

The scalping knife was never sharper, seldom bloodier. The torch was put to cabin after cabin. At mid-day and at midnight the flames which consumed the scattered evidences of civilization west of the Ohio river leaped skyward. The fierce war-whoop rang defiantly from Detroit south to the settlements in Kentucky and no white man was safe. Harmless traders, and peaceable hunters as well as settlers were murdered and their scalps hung high on the lodges of the Delawares, Shawnees, Chippewas, Wyandots, and all the tribes between the Wabash river and the Allegheny mountains.

And all the while the British at Detroit were urging the Indians on, and all the while the authorities of the American government were urging moderation on Wayne's part and trying hopelessly to bring about peace.

Some peace commissioners who were sent to treat with the Indians were at first received kindly, but without warning, a few days later, slain.

News traveled far less rapidly in those days than now. A family might at midnight hear the redskins' dreadful yells and die fleeing from the fierce savages, even while flames devoured their home. But neighbors only a few miles distant would continue to dwell in supposed security, knowing nothing of the outrage, and so only the more readily fall victims of the same ferocious Indian band a little later.

Indeed, it is not remarkable that Return and John had felt little fear among the Indians, while living so far from the frontier that news of the terrible tragedies along the border did not reach them. Their entire plan for the future had been from the first to make the redskins their friends. They had, with some rather serious exceptions, in which they were not at fault,

145

succeeded admirably until Lone-Elk incited Captain Pipe's people to hostility. But now, even had both the boys been at their cabin, and seemingly at peace with every tribe, as they had once been, they could not have failed to discover evidence of the warlike activity about them. They would not only have seen but, very likely, have felt, the increasing hostility of every redman the vast wilds contained.

No longer did the head men, such as Chief Hopocon or Captain Pipe, seek to restrain the bloodthirsty young warriors. They were allowed full sway. Treaties still fresh in their minds, such as that fixing the Cuyahoga and the portage trail as a definite boundary between the white men and their red brethren, were forgotten or no more regarded than the leaves which drifted before the autumn winds.

The arrival of John Jerome; bound hand and foot, at the Delaware town on the lake was the signal for an outburst of ferocious savage hilarity, by no means comforting to that young gentleman.

Twice had John attempted to escape from the five young bucks — Indians scarcely older than himself — and each time had he failed. First he had tried to buy his liberty and exerted every effort to prevail upon the youthful braves to give him his freedom, to give him at least a chance for it, a start of three yards, then the use of his hands and feet and no start at all. His endeavors and his pleading were all fruitless.

Determined to escape, then, John made a bold-dash while the little party was on the march; but the strap which held him was strong, and he was stopped in a moment. His second attempt to get away was scarcely more successful. The Indians had paused to rest and refresh themselves beside a little lake which lay but a few miles from the Delaware town. One of the fellows, the one who held the long strip of rawhide tied to the captive's neck, lay down on the beach to drink. For a moment he released his hold on the strap and instantly John took advantage of it. But he ran only a few rods before two of the braves caught him, and the punishment they and the others administered was severe. Then it was that the prisoner's feet as well as his hands were bound and so was he dragged into the village at last.

In vain did John look about for Fishing Bird, for Gentle Maiden or some of the other Delawares who had been especially friendly in the past. Fishing Bird, of course, was not there, and Gentle Maiden remained out of sight. That she felt sympathy for the prisoner, however, is certain. She saw to it that proper food was carried to him, and exerted all her influence to prevent harm from coming to him. Especially did she urge that the sentence of death for witchcraft should not be executed until the return of Captain Pipe, who was gone to the Delaware town on the Muskingum.

As Lone-Elk, also, was away, and as he had a strong personal interest in the infliction of the punishment the Little Paleface must suffer, no more was done to end the captive's life at once. But one by one the Delawares informed John of what he must expect. Some told him his fate would be death at the stake. Others said that Lone-Elk would end everything with one mighty blow with the same hatchet that had caused Big Buffalo's death.

Even these gloomy assurances, however, did not alarm poor John so much as the wild hostility he saw everywhere about him — nearly all the Indians in war paint, their war-whoops ringing out at every hour of the day and night, as they contemplated the extinction of both the settlers and later the whole Paleface army, gathering as they knew, to march against them. Much of the threatening demonstration was due to the keen zest of the younger savages. In the absence of their chief they were under no restraint and the ferocious delight with which they scented from afar the expected fighting was but a part of their nature.

Day after day slipped by and Captain Pipe did not return. Confined in a rude hut, without fire and without comforts of any kind, excepting sufficient food, such as it was, John Jerome suffered both in body and in spirit. But he was to suffer more later. Indeed, each day brought its additional burdens of grief and pain.

Constantly watched as he was, the sorrowful boy found not one reason to believe that a chance to escape might come to him, and now was anxiety for his own safety more than doubled by the conviction forced upon him that Return Kingdom was gone forever—murdered, tortured, shot from ambush. He knew not how his life had been taken, but the certain evidence that Ree was dead was presented to him in the course of a night of savage barbarity the like of which few white men ever had equal opportunities of seeing.

It was late in the afternoon of an ideal Indian summer day that Lone-Elk returned to the Delaware town. He brought bullets and this time powder also. Only a shrug of his bare shoulders marked his interest in the news when told that the "witch" was captured; that Little Paleface was even at the moment safely held captive beyond all possibility of escape.

He did not so much as go to see and gloat over the unhappy prisoner; but a murderous gleam came in his eyes and he told Neohaw and several others that the stake and the fire would be the "witch's" portion when Captain Pipe came. He would not execute the death sentence before the chief's return, for then they would have a celebration which would be a lesson to all the Palefaces for many days to come, just as the burning of the "White Chief," Crawford, had been.

Nevertheless Lone-Elk quickly laid his plans to torture and torment the young captive, and to instill in the minds of all the Delawares a hatred of every Paleface, and a belief in the certain ease with which their country might be rid of them. He arranged a war dance. Every warrior, every buck and brave in the village answered his summons. Gentle Maiden guessed at once the meaning of it all, as in the early twilight the fighting men of her father's people began to gather. It was useless for her to remonstrate, and as the fierce, sharp cries that accompanied the horrid dance swelled in volume and in number, John himself was scarcely more apprehensive of the outcome than was she.

Bound and round the campfire the savages danced. Their contortions of face and body, their violent shrieks and awful fervor were terrible to look upon. Fiercest of all was Lone-Elk. Louder than all the others was the war-whoop of the Seneca, and at midnight he had wrought to the highest pitch of bloodthirsty ardor every Delaware participating in the horrible revelry.

"Come!" called the outcast loudly at last, "Come! Will the Delawares close their eyes in sleep when so near them is a house of the Palefaces? A house that will draw others to it till the forests of the Indians are all cut down and they themselves driven away and killed? Come! Who will come with Lone-Elk!"

A fierce chorus of war cries greeted his words. Drunk with excitement, the Delawares paused not to consider. With terrible yells they surged after the Seneca and like a shrieking band of fiends hurried rapidly through the moonlit forest.

"Hold! Let the Delawares bring the Paleface witch!" cried Lone-Elk. "Let the murderer of the brave Big Buffalo see the nest where birds of his kind are hatched go up in fire!"

No sooner said than done. A dozen of the fiercest of the band, mad with the passions that had been aroused within them, rushed back and in five minutes came dragging John Jerome after them. By a rope around his body, and by another about his neck, they both drove and pulled him. Their awful yells could have been heard for miles.

Following the portage trail to its end and crossing the river, the savages broke into the clearing about the cabin a little further on at a run. Up the hill they went and with whooping and yelling of impassioned fury they attacked the cabin, so humble, so quiet and so home-like and unoffending in its appearance that its destruction seemed the foulest crime in all of border warfare's awful annals.

With tomahawks the door was beaten in, though but to have pulled the string would have raised the latch, and the mad race of pillage and plunder began. Everything breakable was thrown down and destroyed. Table, stools, bedding and all the little conveniences that Ree and John had been at such pains to plan and construct were thrown indiscriminately about.

"Let the witch burn his own foul nest," the Seneca yelled in his native tongue, but the captive, trembling with anger and sickened by the awful scenes he was compelled to witness, understood and drew back. In vain two Delawares who held him sought to force him to take and apply the torch that a third held out. They burned his bare hands, set fire to his clothing and his hair, but to no purpose. He could not fight, but he could resist if it killed him, and resist John did, let the consequences be what they might.

"Ugh! Ugh!" loudly ejaculated one of the older Indians impatiently, at last, and grabbing the burning hickory bark from the one who tried vainly to make the prisoner take it, he carried it quickly into the lean-to stable.

In an instant the dry hay and fodder were in flames. In another minute the fire had reached the cabin. Soon the terrible glare filled all the clearing and while the home the boy pioneers had held so dear, and all the things within it which long association made them fondly cherish, turned black, then red and yielded at last to the crackling, roaring destroyer, the Indians danced about in savage celebration, brandishing tomahawks and scalping knives, yelling and shrieking like the untamed demons that they were.

CHAPTER XXII – THE MAN IN THE RAVINE

Very little time indeed was required for Return Kingdom to make clear to Fishing Bird the work he wished to do. The Delaware was decidedly surprised to learn that a white man, or men, of whom he knew nothing, were encamped near the Cuyahoga and he also exhibited the liveliest interest in the information Ree gave him concerning the two men murdered at the salt springs.

The probability that John Jerome had been captured, however, interested the Indian more than all else, though it distressed him, too. Repeatedly he shook his head with an air of utmost gravity and regret.

Gen. Wayne was a man who did things. Once his plans were formed, their execution went ahead without a moment's unnecessary delay, and in a very short space of time he had caused men to be detailed to accompany Kingdom and his loyal friend.

The boy's request that Sergeant Quayle be sent with him was promptly granted and that good-natured son of Erin with three others, all experienced woodsmen, gladly undertook the duty assigned them. They agreed with Kingdom, too, that a large force of men would not be needed, and that by care a small party would be able to accomplish more than a greater number. They would be far less likely to attract attention or invite an attack from ambush.

Late in the afternoon the well-armed band set out. By common consent Kingdom was given general command, though he took counsel always with the others. Only one circumstance marred his perfect confidence in the expedition. This was the distrustful manner in which two of the woodsmen constantly regarded Fishing Bird. They were Indian haters and Indian fighters. They could "see no good in 'ary a single red mother's son of 'em," as one of them expressed it, "and didn't care who knowed it."

The Sergeant, however, was more charitably inclined. Being of buoyant spirits, too, when somewhat relieved of the camp's restraints, he kept everyone in a good humor with his droll remarks.

Even over the badly decomposed bodies of the two unfortunate men, killed at the "big lick," his manner was the same.

"Sure, they'd ha' be'an far better presarved if put in the brine! An' so much o' it, handy like, 'tis a shame, it is!" said he.

But notwithstanding, Quayle, as well as all the others, was much affected by the awful sight the removal of the brush heap disclosed. Ree knew from John's description just where to look for the bodies of the murdered men, and he hoped to find something that his friend might have overlooked, which would reveal the men's identities. Sergeant Quayle and the woodsmen had also been anxious to see if they could not tell who the unfortunates were, and it was for these reasons that the springs were visited, though they lay somewhat away from the direct trail.

Nothing did the little party find to shed any light on the mysterious murder. The older woodsmen declared that both the dead men must have come from some distant point. If either had belonged anywhere in the vicinity of the Ohio river, they would have seen them at some time, they were sure. Sergeant Quayle was of the opinion, from the dress and general appearance of the murdered pair, that they had come from some of the British posts in the Northwest, probably Detroit. Yet he expressed the belief that Indians had committed the murder, and only when Kingdom reminded him of the evidence afforded by the pair of gloves that had been found, did he say:

"Leastwise, we'll agree to this, lad; savages done it. White men or red men, they was blackhearted savages that done such a dirty deed!"

The party spent a night in the vicinity of the salt springs. Though regretting the least delay, and anxious always to be pushing on, Kingdom was greatly interested in the evidences of civilization having at one time had a foothold at the "lick," as John had been. He was fortunate in learning more about the matter than Jerome had learned, however, for one of the woodsmen—a great, broad-shouldered young fellow, whose name, oddly enough, was Small,—knew much about the springs.

In camp at night he told the others how, several years earlier, Gen. Samuel H. Parsons had come from Connecticut and attempted to establish a salt factory at the place. He undertook to purchase twenty-five thousand acres of land, embracing the springs and the territory about them, and expected to reap a great fortune. He was greatly disappointed in the quantity of salt the water contained, but might have carried out his plan, anyway, had it not been that, in returning from the springs to the east, he was drowned by the upsetting of his canoe at the Beaver falls. The purchase of the great tract he had intended buying, was, therefore, never completed.

"But as a rule, lad, ye'll note as ye go through life," said the Sergeant to Ree—he nearly always addressed his words to Kingdom "as a rule, ye'll note that parsons are more partial to poultry than to salt. Still, ye'll do well to tie to the parsons, Lord bless 'em! It's a preacher I'd ha' be'an me ownsilf but fur——"

The Sergeant left his exclamation unfinished and with a sigh, which was also a chuckle, lay down and drew his blanket close about him.

Kingdom planned to lead his party directly to the cabin on the Cuyahoga. He was hoping he would find John Jerome in that neighborhood or in hiding at the old poplar, even while he told himself how little ground he had for such a thought.

Men coming to Wayne's camp from Fort Pitt had brought word that John had not been there, and where to look for him, excepting near the cabin, or among the Delawares, Ree did not know. He was depending on Fishing Bird to obtain information for him, however, and repeatedly, on the journey west, the Indian would go a long distance from the others of the party to find, if possible, some wandering redskins who might be able to give him news of the capture of the lad they sought.

153

Although at no time was the Delaware in any way successful, he never failed to rejoin Ree and his white friends at night. In every way, both then and later, he proved himself thoroughly trustworthy and loyal, despite the daily predictions of Jim Small that he would turn up missing when he was most wanted, and be found hostile when his friendship was most desired.

The march through the forest wilds was interrupted by no incident of importance. Ree had left his horse at Wayne's encampment, as he had no wish to ride while others walked, and, under the circumstances, the mare would be a hindrance. Rapid progress was made by the "expedition," as Sergeant Quayle always called the little band of six, however, and the increasing severity of the weather was almost the only hardship of the undertaking.

At the middle of an afternoon much pleasanter than the raw, cold days which had preceded it, the expedition reached a point only a few miles from the clearing and the river. A council of war was held and it was decided that Ree and Fishing Bird should go forward to look for John at the cabin, while Sergeant Quayle and the others turned off to the north to await their report at a certain rocky ledge of which both Kingdom and the woodsmen knew.

The chief reason for this action was the secrecy which must be observed to prevent knowledge of the presence of so large a party reaching the mysterious camp in the gully. The camp itself would be inspected under cover of darkness and a decision could then be reached concerning the best time and manner of surprising the murderers, and effecting their capture. If it were found that the camp seemed permanently occupied, and the occupants intending to stay indefinitely, they would be allowed to rest in supposed security while John Jerome was being located.

Ree had seen from the first that the men who accompanied him were more keenly interested in the lead mine than anything else. He would rather have made the finding of John Jerome the first object to be achieved, but he gave way to the wishes of the Sergeant in this instance, and now he and Fishing Bird hastened on to the cabin.

Cautiously Kingdom and the Delaware approached the clearing. The sun shone lazily, the air, though cool, was soft and still. Peace seemed everywhere. It was hard to believe the reverse was true. And then came the shock.

From the edge of the woods Ree saw the awful work Lone-Elk and his warriors had done. Not a muscle of his face moved. Though even Fishing Bird sorrowfully shook his head and put his arm before his eyes to shut out the most unhappy scene, the boy remained cool and collected. No sign of the tempest of grief and boiling anger that raged within him was visible on the surface. With surprise the Delaware observed his calm demeanor and heard him say:

"Whose work this is, Fishing Bird, we don't know. Just what has been done, though, we can plainly see. I am afraid it means something worse. So what I want you to do, good Fishing Bird, is to hurry to the Delaware town. Hurry to the village and learn anything and all you can about what has happened to Little Paleface. Whether the Delawares know much, or nothing, come to me at the rocks where I am to meet my friends, tomorrow morning. Come early, Fishing Bird, and bring good news if you can. Bring bad news if you must. But most of all don't fail me."

"Every word Fishing Bird understands," the Indian answered, and in another minute was gone.

For a very short time Ree lingered at the clearing's edge. Tears came to his eyes, now that he was alone, when he looked at the fire-stained chimney rising like a spectre above the ruin of ashes around it, — the only thing left of his home. Quickly, however, he wiped the evidence of his sorrow from his face. He glanced around for old Neb, the cart horse, but saw nothing of the animal. "They've taken him too, no doubt," he thought, and his heart grew more bitter and his face more stern, as he turned away.

The ease with which Kingdom traversed the forest, up hill and down hill, and his familiarity with the country for miles around, enabled him to reach the meeting place at the rocky ledge almost as soon as Sergeant Quayle and his companions. Briefly he told them what he had seen. They asked questions which he could not answer, as he had not minutely inspected the clearing, but he did not tell them his reason for not having done so, though he knew it well. It was because he could not bear to undertake the heartbreaking task.

"Anyway," said Sergeant Quayle, "our business tonight is t' see this queer camp ye've tould us of, an' hear what the redskin tells in the mornin'."

So were plans made accordingly and after a cold supper all hands set out stealthily to inspect the haunt of the mysterious man in the gully. Ree led the way, nor was his task difficult. The light of a small campfire was seen reflected on the branches of the trees, even before the ravine was reached.

Stooping low, and taking every step with care, all five approached the edge of the bluff. For a few minutes nothing more than the small blaze could be seen. But the fire had lately been replenished with fresh wood and, with this evidence that some one was near, the watchers were content to wait.

Soon a man came into view. He carried several slices of meat and, sprinkling them freely with salt from a pouch at his belt, prepared to broil them. Little did he suspect how intently his every movement was scrutinized, for he mumbled to himself, and spread his great hands out to the warmth of the blaze, as if he had no thought but to enjoy the meal he was preparing. When the meat was cooked he ate greedily, then disappearing for a few seconds, returned with more. This he disposed of in the same way.

For perhaps half an hour he continued to sit near the fire, but rising in a regretful manner, at last, he covered the embers with ashes, then disappeared and returned no more.

Until far into the night Ree and his four companions remained watching, then cautiously withdrew. The moonlight filtered through the leafless branches of the trees and the air was very frosty. For warmth and rest Kingdom led the party to the hollow whitewood. Here a conference was held and the decision reached to return to the camp in the gully just before daybreak.

Whether the others slept Ree did not know. They all were wrapped in their blankets and very quiet. But he knew that he did not sleep, nor could he had he tried. The loss of John, the burned cabin, the whole sorrowful end of all the bright hopes of a few weeks before kept his thoughts too unhappily occupied, and he was glad of the darkness that it concealed his grief and pain.

Sometime before dawn Sergeant Quayle stretched himself and sat up. Kingdom did likewise and the others were also soon astir. With the same care as before, they moved upon the haunted ravine, and chose their places, each a little distance from the others, but all where they could hurry down the steep hillside at a moment's notice.

The sun was just rising as the tenant of the lonely camp came suddenly into the light, stretching himself and yawning.

The click of the Sergeant's rifle as he cocked it was the signal, and it sounded loud enough. Silently, swiftly and almost noiselessly the five men descended the bluff, and, almost before the murderer's yawn permitted his mouth to close, it was open again, but this time in extraordinary astonishment. He was surrounded by stern, strange faces.

CHAPTER XXIII – ONE MYSTERY CLEARED AWAY

It was daylight when with parting war-whoops the Indians left the scene of the terrible fire they had kindled, dragging John Jerome by the thongs which bound him. But they took with them flames which threatened even greater danger to the Paleface boy – the fires of excitement, hate and merciless cruelty which the night's barbarities had kindled in their brains. John realized this full well. Though the savages had been rough and brutal in their treatment of him before, now they were still more so. No indignity, no suffering was too great to be inflicted upon him.

Little wonder is it that on his own account poor John wished for but two things – the slightest opportunity to escape, or the end of it all quickly. Only the thoughts of Return, and how his friend would be searching for him everywhere, as soon as news reached his ears, buoyed up the wretched lad's drooping spirits and gave him strength to endure the cruelties heaped on his defenseless head.

Tired out after their night's carousal, most of the savages lay down to rest upon their arrival at the village, and John was allowed also to sink into a troubled sleep, though watched constantly. It was about noon when he fully awoke, to find that something out of the ordinary was taking place. By degrees he discovered what it was, learned that Captain Pipe had returned and that explanations were being made concerning the burning of the cabin.

Lone-Elk took upon himself the whole responsibility for the offense. The Little Paleface was a witch, he declared, and his brother, the White Fox, was a spy upon the Indians, and on the pretext of befriending Fishing Bird, had gone to Wayne's camp to carry word of the movements of the Delawares.

The Seneca would have put the loyalty of Fishing Bird himself to the Delawares in question had he dared to do so, but he gained his point without it; gained all he sought – praise for his own loyalty to the cause of the Indians as a whole; no censure for the pillage and destruction of the white boys' cabin, and last and greatest of all, the assurance that the captive, Little Paleface, would be put to death.

Let him be burned at the stake, Lone-Elk argued. Some of the younger Delawares had never seen a prisoner suffer by fire. It would warm their blood and teach them how to punish their enemies.

"By fire, then, let the witch be killed," Captain Pipe had ordered, and the terrible sentence reached John Jerome in his guarded hut a little later.

Four warriors came. They roughly stripped him of all clothing excepting his fringed buckskin trousers, and painted his face and body black. Thus he was left for the time, as the hour of his torture was to be the following morning. But he was told to prepare for death and formed bluntly that with the rising of another sun he would bid farewell to earth forever.

In vain did John ask to see Captain Pipe. The chief would not go near him. He asked for Gentle Maiden, knowing that she would intercede for him if she could. No word was taken to her. He asked for Neohaw. The old medicine-man came. He heard the lad's appeal, and shook his head.

"Neohaw can do nothing," he declared. "Lone-Elk is in favor with all the Delawares and with their great chief, Hopocon. No one can help the Little Paleface. Neohaw believes not that the Paleface brother killed Big Buffalo. Yet all the Delawares have harkened to the tale of the Seneca and the white boy must die. Let him then go bravely to the fire. Let him sing boldly to the last the death songs that his fathers taught him."

John thanked the aged Indian for his sympathy and said no more. He did feel better, somehow, to know that there was one friend left in the village, where so many times he had been received with greatest favor in days gone by, and resolved that if die he must, it would be bravely.

Something very like tears, however, dimmed his eyes as he thought of his unhappy end. He held them back with an effort and, lest they come again, and be taken as evidence of fear or cowardice, he prayed for strength to meet the awful fate he must suffer like a man. He breathed a prayer for comfort for Ree Kingdom and for the dear ones in far-away Connecticut, when the news of his death should reach them.

It was night now. The Indians made the most of it. Their war cries, as once again they engaged in the terrible dance, led, as always, by the bloodthirsty Seneca, were frightful. But to John Jerome a peace which passeth understanding had come, and with thoughts of all the happy days his young life, so soon to close, had known, and in his heart a trusting faith that One who died for others would be with him to the end, he fell at last into soothing, restful slumber.

At dawn John awoke. The village was quiet. The two savages who stood guard over him seemed to be the only ones not still asleep, save for a trio of squaws rekindling the fires before their wigwams. The air was chill and raw, but crows were cawing lustily, and a bluejay screeched his harsh song near by. Soon the sun rose, pale but clear. It was a pleasant morning to be alive, a most gloomy one to die.

Patiently the prisoner of the Delawares awaited the executioners. They soon would come, he thought, and nerved himself to meet them without a tremor. His lip quivered the least bit and a lump came in his throat, but outwardly he was so calm that the Indians watching him marveled at his courage, and told one another in whispers that witches were more than human.

The morning went quickly by. Expecting each minute to see Lone-Elk and others coming for him, time seemed to John to go both slow and fast; slow, that no one came; fast, because each minute was so precious. Hope had not wholly left him, either. It might be, even now, he thought, that Neohaw or Gentle Maiden, or maybe Long-Hair or Little Wolf, had successfully interceded in his behalf.

At last two Indians came to relieve those who guarded the prisoner. The Delawares were stirring about in numbers now. John asked the new guards for food and it was brought to him. Then Neohaw came. In a kindly way he told the boy that the time of the burning had been changed and the torture fire would not be lighted until night. Against Lone-Elk's wishes, Captain Pipe had decided on this, as he had no wish to participate in the terrible festivities. He planned to go away near evening and leave everything to the Seneca.

All day the more cruel of the Delawares exhibited their impatience. All day squaws were busy adding to the collection of wood about the burning-post, set firmly in the ground at the edge of the collection of huts and wigwams that comprised the town. Between the logs of his prison John could plainly see all that went on.

It was late in the afternoon. Night's shades were deepening. The sun had nearly sunk from view and a soft, golden light rested for a time on the bosom of the little lake.

With a glad cry an Indian came leaping into the village. Fishing Bird it was, and his joy at being safe at home once more was great. In a moment, however, his happiness vanished. In a trice he discovered the burning-post and the fagots piled near it. He guessed its meaning instantly, and his fears were immediately confirmed as he made inquiry.

Captain Pipe was just leaving the village but stayed a few seconds to give Fishing Bird greeting. He listened gravely to the younger Indian's plea that the Little Paleface be spared. He shook his head. Then Fishing Bird told of the rapid ride Return Kingdom had made through the woods to save a Delaware's life, and called Long-Hair and Little Wolf to tell of the part they had had in that undertaking.

"A council shall be held. The Delawares will give the one accused of witchcraft a fair trial," said the chief at last. "If then it is found that, as a witch, the Little Paleface killed a warrior of the Delawares, he must suffer the penalty. Fishing Bird can ask nothing more."

Very soberly the friendly Indian approached the place of the white boy's confinement and told him that for the present his life was spared.

John's happiness in seeing the loyal fellow once again, and in having another friend at hand, was inexpressible. Soon he had learned all that the Delaware could tell him concerning Ree and what the latter had been doing.

"One thing, then, Fishing Bird, you must do for me," he said. "Let Ree Kingdom know that I am to have a trial. Get Captain Pipe to let you bring him and his friends here."

"Fishing Bird will bring them. Tell nobody," the Indian whispered, and withdrew.

Before the coming of another day the Indian friend of the boy pioneers had left the village. He had found that the time of the council the Delawares would hold to place Little Paleface on trial would be the following afternoon. The torture fire would be lighted in the evening, if the boy was found guilty, as was very certain to be the case. It was with great news to tell and many conflicting thoughts in mind, therefore, that he sped through the woods to meet Return Kingdom at the spot agreed upon.

Thus while Fishing Bird hastened to the meeting place from one point, Ree was making his way toward the same ledge of rocks from another. Without the least difficulty the lone occupant of the mysterious camp had been captured and taken away. While Jim Small and another of the woodsmen watched the camp from the bushes to surprise and make prisoners of any confederates of the fellow, should such put in an appearance, Sergeant Quayle and the fourth of his squad held the murderer in close quarters at the hollow whitewood. Search of the camp would not be made, it was agreed, until Kingdom's return with Fishing Bird.

Ree and the Delaware reached the place of meeting at about the same time. As the redskin came up, Kingdom searched his face anxiously for some clue to the tidings he brought. It was vain to do so. Indian-like, he could conceal his thoughts completely and he wanted the pleasure of telling what he had accomplished before its substance was surmised.

He soon did tell, however, all that had happened and very soberly, indeed, did Ree receive the news. How glad he was that Fishing Bird had reached the village so opportunely need not be told. The great question was what could be done to rescue John Jerome?

"We'll ask the Sergeant what he thinks about it," said Kingdom as the Delaware told more fully of the desperate situation their friend was in. "Come, we must hurry. There'll be not a minute to lose."

Another surprise awaited Ree when the old poplar was reached.

"Whist! The dirty British pig has tould iverything!" whispered Sergeant Quayle, meeting Kingdom and the Indian at the edge of the thicket. "A foine thing it is, too, so it is!" And with these words the disgusted Irishman led the way forward.

Within the hollow tree there lay a great bulk of a fellow groveling on the leaf-strewn earth, bewailing his fate, pleading for mercy, and altogether making of himself a most miserable, loathsome spectacle.

"Oh, if I'd knowed it would come to this!" he blubbered. "Don't let them punish me! Oh, kind gentlemen, save me! Let me go away and sin no more! Won't some one speak a kind word to me?"

The abject fear of the craven, now that his crime had found him out, would have been pitiable had his whole manner not been so utterly contemptible.

Giving little heed to the guilty wretch, however, Ree at once apprised the Sergeant of the news Fishing Bird had brought and the latter was immediately sent to summon Jim Small and his companions for a conference.

While he was gone Sergeant Quayle told, with many expletives and many invectives against the British, the confession the murderer had made. The fellow's name, it developed, was Lobb. He had been connected in an unofficial way with the British garrison at Detroit and had served a number of times as a go-between for the English officers in certain of their more or less secret dealings with the Indians. In consequence of these services he was chosen to accompany two men sent to encourage hostilities among the savages to the south of Lake Erie and as near the border of the American settlements as they should deem it prudent to go.

The party traveled by canoe, Lobb had said, and coasting along the southern shore of Lake Erie, readied and ascended the Cuyahoga river. In the course of this trip they fell in with Lone-Elk, roaming the woods alone, as his frequent custom was. The Seneca was not unknown to the men, for he had visited Detroit and offered his services to the British when forced to flee from his home among his own people.

For various reasons, but principally because they feared some news of their presence would reach Fort Pitt or Gen. Wayne, the men concluded to do all their business with the Indians of the locality through Lone-Elk. He would distribute their bounty, the powder and the bullets they brought, also gold for those who cared for it.

Not long had the men been in the vicinity when they decided to visit the salt springs of which they had heard a great deal. To conceal their identity they concluded, also, that they would make some salt while there, pretending that such was the sole purpose of their presence.

It was at the springs that Lobb's cupidity got the better of his natural cowardice and what little decency he possessed. With a view to obtaining the gold in the party's possession, and thinking then to escape to the east in disguise, he concealed himself and shot both his comrades just as they were preparing to leave the springs. To convey the impression that Indians had done the awful deed he scalped both men. Then, filled with fear lest the bodies be found before he could get away, he had dragged them into the woods and covered them with brush.

"Well, why did he hang around here? What did he say about the lead mine?" asked Ree, as the Sergeant finished.

164

"Sure, it's all the farther he wint with his black yarn, fer with 'ye dirty cur, ye!' I give him a push an' a shove an' he landed where he's still layin', hard an' fast ferninst the ground there."

Lobb was questioned further by Kingdom immediately. The boy believed he saw in the loathsome creature's story reason to believe that the Delawares had been grievously deceived by the Seneca.

Whining and groaning, the self-confessed murderer continued his story. He had been afraid to go on east from the springs, he said, and made all haste back to the Cuyahoga, where he and his companions had established headquarters in a small cave, originally pointed out to them by Lone-Elk.

From here he dared move in no direction. He was afraid to return to Detroit—afraid to go east, west, north or south. Knowing of the presence of the two boy pioneers, a few miles away, his fears were greatly increased lest they discover him and guess his guilty secret. Day after day, then, he had lived in the hole in the hillside, coming out only at night to prepare food, or when forced to go in search of fresh meat.

Imploring mercy and begging for freedom, the fellow concluded his statement.

"You've told everything, have you!" Kingdom asked with as little harshness as his feelings would permit.

"Aye, master, aye—everything," Lobb whined.

"So it was you, then, who supplied Lone-Elk with lead and bullets, and his story of a lead mine was a story and nothing more?" the boy demanded.

"I guess so. I don't know anything about a lead mine, master. Truly I don't know anything about it. I do remember though, come to think, that Lone-Elk said once that I was his lead mine and I must look out that the Palefaces didn't find it out."

"You hear that, Sergeant?" exclaimed Ree, with some excitement. "Now let us see whether that sneaking Seneca will continue to rule the Delawares!"

CHAPTER XXIV – WHO KILLED BIG BUFFALO

Even before Kingdom finished questioning the murderer, Fishing Bird had come up bringing the two woodsmen from the gully. All three were quickly informed of Lobb's confession and of the discovery of John Jerome and the great danger surrounding him. The entire party looked to Ree for a suggestion.

"We've got to act and act quickly," the lad said in a low tone. "If Fishing Bird will be our escort, I propose that we go to the Delaware town as fast as we can go. If Captain Pipe can be made to understand that Lone-Elk has deceived the Delawares in one way, we can, with Fishing Bird's help, and Lobb's confession, bring him to his senses about this witchcraft business."

"Lone-Elk's a bad 'un. He killed a Seneca and had to leave home," put in Lobb, who had listened attentively.

"Huh!" snorted Sergeant Quayle. "Cain killed Abel an' had to leave home; but he didn't go bush-whackin' two men from behind!"

"And what about Mr. Lobb, anyhow! We can't leave him, once we've had the pleasure of his company?" put in Jim Small, with sarcasm.

"Take him along," said another of the woodsmen.

"Yes, that is what I had in mind," Ree answered. "He can tell Pipe what he has told us. But we must be moving, men! It's a long tramp and time's flying!"

Without loss of time the party got under way. No one questioned the wisdom of Kingdom's plan, although, if the truth were known, two of the men at least, looked for a lively scrimmage as a result of the undertaking. But they did not falter. Indeed, it is a question if they did not rather relish the prospect of a brush with the Delawares. Lobb was completely disarmed but he was not bound.

"I give ye my word, master, I'll not try get-tin' away," he said.

"Whist! Give me yer chances in the hereafter; one's as good as 'tother," retorted the Sergeant contemptuously, and then informed the murderer further that the slightest attempt on his part would result in his being shot first and asked as to the meaning of it afterward.

The fellow made some very humble answer but he grew decidedly thoughtful and rather sullen as the marchers hurried rapidly through the woods. There was a gleam of satisfaction in his eyes, too, when the party passed the clearing and saw only a heap of ashes and the chimney where the boys' cabin had stood. He was thinking. He was planning to betray his captors and with Lone-Elk's help to turn the tables upon them. How well he succeeded will soon be told, for now comes a part of this history which all participants therein remembered throughout their lives, and which left its impress upon the people of Captain Pipe's town long after the village itself had ceased to be.

The day was bright and clear. Though not warm, neither was it very cold, and the south wind which sighed in the leafless branches of the trees and gently rippled the waters of the little lake seemed soft as velvet. The Delawares were in fine spirits. With savage rapture they looked forward to the terrible celebration the night would bring.

From the lower towns on the Muskingum Captain Pipe had brought encouraging news of Indian successes along the border and almost without exception his warriors were enthusiastic for the final conflict with Wayne's "Legion," which, they believed, would not be long in coming. They felt perfect confidence as to the outcome. They had seen his raw recruits. They did not know then that "Mad Anthony" had no intention of marching upon them until his troops were trained. This and much else they learned in time and to their sorrow.

But there was another reason for a feeling of happiness in the Delaware town, and particularly was Lone-Elk, the Seneca, in a good humor. This very day there had arrived the two warriors whom Captain Pipe had sent with an offering of white wampum to the friends of him Lone-Elk had slain. Not as compensation, not as damages for the injury done, had the gift of wampum pure and white been sent, but as a plea for forgiveness; as a symbol of the slayer's penitence and sorrow.

It was somewhat unusual for an offering of peace to be accepted so long after the crime had been committed, and it was known, too, that Lone-Elk's offense had been particularly cruel. So was there very good reason for the Seneca to shake hands with his Delaware friends and receive their congratulations.

Captain Pipe thought the outcast seemed less truly sorry for his crime than he should have been. He little liked the haughty manner in which the one so lately restored to a place of honor and respect in his own tribe and nation bore himself. Perhaps he thought, also, that the Seneca was less appreciative of the service rendered him than he should have been. Nevertheless he gave the bold warrior his hand and told him that, though he was now free to return to his own people, he would have a place of honor among the Delawares as long as he chose to remain with them.

John Jerome heard by degrees of what had happened. He wondered if the Seneca would not now be less bitter toward him, and more fair and honorable. But he was grievously disappointed. Lone-Elk showed himself more hostile, if possible, than before; more keen to carry out his plot to avenge the pretended killing of Big Buffalo by witchcraft; more intense in his hatred.

As he learned just how matters stood, John's only hope for escape lay in Return Kingdom and the men of whom Fishing Bird had told him. He knew they would attempt to rescue him, but seeing how greatly they were out-numbered, fear of the outcome worried him more and more. It was bad enough for him to suffer, he declared within himself, again and again, without dragging Ree and others to the same fate.

The hour of the council to inquire into the guilt of the prisoner arrived. The Indians assembled and once again John found himself in the long, low bark house where always in the past he had met the Delawares as friends.

Captain Pipe and every buck and warrior of the village was in attendance; but more conspicuous than any of them, more proud and more erect, was Lone-Elk, the Seneca. In his hands he held the hatchet brought by him from the cornfield of the young Palefaces, the hatchet with which, he said, Big Buffalo had been slain. It was the evidence that-would substantiate his story of the witch's work.

Captain Pipe stated the purpose of the council briefly and quietly. Then he informed the prisoner that the Delawares would hear what he had to say, but urged him to confess his sin and not, on the eve of death, be guilty of a lie.

With face and body blackened, his hands bound to a stick behind him, the accused boy arose. He tried to be bold and fearless, but, though he looked the Indians squarely in the eyes, he could not speak as he wished to do. His voice did not falter, but the words seemed somehow to refuse to come.

The charge against him was false, he said, and time would prove it. Never except in fair fight had he harmed any Indian. He would leave it to Captain Pipe to judge if he had not always conducted himself as a friend of the Delawares. He reminded them how, only the past winter, he had brought their women and children food while the able men were away for the fighting that had taken place. With a suppressed sigh as he saw how little impression he had made on the hostile faces round him, John sat down.

In an instant Lone-Elk was on his feet. With head thrown back and flashing eyes he repeated the story of the cloud which drifted over the lake — repeated again the whole miserable tale he had told so many times before. Then he exhibited the hatchet taken from the shock of corn on which a crow of most strange appearance had the same day been seen.

"Lone-Elk well knows who put the tomahawk where he got it, Captain Pipe," the prisoner found courage to say. But for doing so the warriors beside him smartly rapped his head with their knuckles, and the Seneca gave him a look of hate so fierce, so vindictive it startled him.

"The white brother's time for speech is over," the chief made answer coldly, and Lone-Elk now resuming his seat, he said: "The Delawares will hear any who wish to speak further."

A travel-stained figure glided swiftly from the door to Captain Pipe's side and spoke to him in quick, low tones that few could hear. It was Fishing Bird.

"There are Palefaces who wait with a white flag, Palefaces who wish to be heard," the chief announced, in the Delaware tongue. "Fishing Bird may bring them here."

Lone-Elk, with glaring eyes, rose hastily and would have remonstrated but with a kindly, yet imperious wave of his hand Captain Pipe motioned to him to sit down, and he obeyed.

In another minute Return Kingdom, followed by five other white men, stepped into the Council House.

"Captain Pipe," said Kingdom at once, "we have put down our guns and come here without arms to say a few words to the Delawares which they may be surprised to hear. The Delawares are in council and it is a proper time to speak to them. We ask nothing more than that you let us be heard."

"The Delawares will listen to White Fox," the chief answered. "While the council lasts we shall be as friends. When it is over the Paleface brothers may go their way."

"We thank Captain Pipe and all the Delawares," Kingdom answered in clear, loud, friendly tones. "We have come to you with important news. We are received as your friends and we shall be such while in your village. The news we bring will not be pleasant to all of you. For the Delawares have been deceived. There is one here who has led Captain Pipe and many of his people to believe he knew of a secret mine from which he could supply them with much lead and with bullets."

Kingdom paused for an instant, and as he did so Lone-Elk for the first time caught sight of Lobb standing between two of the woodsmen. The look he darted toward the fellow was venomous. There is no doubt but what he thought the Englishman had revealed his secret, then led the white men thither to betray him.

But after the one quick, black look the Seneca seemed quite indifferent to the presence of any of the white men. He concealed his thoughts completely and the Delawares who cast questioning glances toward him were amazed at his composure. Not so with Captain Pipe, however. He had seen on Lone-Elk's brow the awful scowl which came and went so quickly, and to him it spoke volumes.

The pause in Kingdom's speech was very short, and few of the Delawares noticed for a time the effect his words had produced upon their chief. It was not until later that they saw on his face the fixed expression of stony coldness dreaded by all of them.

"There is one among you who has sought to advance himself and his own ambitions by taking advantage of the other Indians," Kingdom went on. "Three white men were sent from Detroit with lead, bullets, powder and gold for the Delawares and other warriors hereabouts. To one Indian only were the lead and bullets and powder given. True, he gave them to the Delawares, but he led them to believe that from a secret mine did he obtain the supplies he brought them. So did he gain power and influence with Captain Pipe's people.

"Now, hear me further. Two of the three men sent by the British to carry stores from Detroit for the Delawares and others have been murdered. The third man killed them. He has confessed his crime and told the whole story of why the Indians did not all share equally in the goods brought for them. This man is here!"

Putting all the emphasis he could muster into his closing sentences, Kingdom signalled his friends as he concluded, and Lobb, trembling and ashy pale, was pushed into the foreground.

"You have heard what I have told the Delawares," Kingdom quietly said. "Do you know if it is true?"

The boy's voice was calm and low, but in the death-like silence of the Council House every word was plainly heard by all, and with intensest interest the savages awaited the answer.

"Yes; it's true," muttered Lobb with a look half of terror, half of appeal and apology toward the Seneca.

"Now point to the one who received the gifts intended for all the Indians, not for him alone," Kingdom commanded.

The murderer looked anxiously about him. He trembled so he could hardly stand, but made no other move.

"Point!" thundered Kingdom. "You know him well!"

"There!" came with a groan from the frightened fellow's lips, and his outstretched finger indicated Lone-Elk.

On the Seneca's face there was an expression so threatening that even Kingdom was alarmed. But he continued his talk boldly.

"He who has deceived the Delawares in one way will deceive them in another. Will they listen when his voice is raised against one who has always been their friend? Will the Delawares allow him to shield himself from suspicion by telling them Big Buffalo was killed by witchcraft? Will they do this? Are the Delawares men? Have they not honor and fairness?"

Kingdom would have said more, and trouble would most certainly have followed, had Captain Pipe permitted it. The Indians were becoming dangerously excited. Jim Small and the other woodsmen, too, were anticipating a row, while John Jerome was on the verge of cheering.

The Delaware chief may have seen what the talk was leading toward; at any rate he quickly rose, commanding silence, and straightway began an address such as his people never before had heard and which no one present could ever forget. His voice was not loud. His tones were those of

172

sorrow rather than anger, but he put into them so much of stern honesty and both reproof and reproach, that his every word was like a knife point. He said:

"There came to the Delawares a fugitive and an outcast. In a moment of anger he had taken the life of one who was raised up over him by his people, the noble Senecas. Still he proved himself in heavy fighting a loyal Indian and a mighty warrior. So did the Delawares open their doors to him. He was given places of honor. When time had passed, and the scar of his crime was old, a present of white wampum was sent to the kindred of the dead Seneca asking their forgiveness.

"This very day have the messengers of the Delawares returned bringing pardon full and free for the stranger among them. Yet this very day do the Delawares learn that they have been treated as children; deceived and misled by him they helped.

"They would have adopted him as one of their own nation, but he has returned their hospitality with lies, their kindest thoughts with evil.

"Of the death of Big Buffalo the Delawares will now inquire among themselves. Witchcraft is an enemy if it exists. The Delawares will learn the truth. But the Seneca must go. Let him leave the town and the hunting grounds of our people forever. Go!"

Waving his right hand haughtily toward Lone-Elk, Captain Pipe concluded, and a flush of anger awful to see came to his face as the Seneca sat still, his whole attitude one of indifference and contempt.

As the chieftain was about to repeat his stern command in even sterner tones, Lone-Elk rose to his feet. For a second or two he toyed with the tomahawk he still held in his hands. Then in insolent tones, both contemptuous and contemptible, and, glaring up and down the rows of faces upturned to him, he said:

"Lone-Elk is a Seneca. Never had he a thought of becoming a Delaware. Why should a Seneca warrior put himself among squaws? For food; for rest. Nothing more. Lone-Elk did not so much as ask that the belt of white wampum be sent to the friends of a Seneca that is dead. He asked no favors of any Delaware. Some of your foolish young men pointed their fingers at Lone-Elk when Big Buffalo was found dead in the bushes by the water. For his amusement Lone-Elk told them of a witch. Like squaws they heard every word. Like children they must hear over and over again and could not have enough. Like children, too, did the Delaware's open their ears and their eyes to hear a legend of a hidden mine of lead. Ugh! A warrior sickens over them and is glad to go."

For a full second the Seneca paused and looked disdainfully about him. There was anger in every Delaware's face.

But suddenly Lone-Elk's demeanor changed. An exclamation of wrath awful to hear burst from his lips.

"There stands the two-tongued Paleface squaw who killed your dead Big Buffalo!" he cried, and shook his fist toward the quaking Lobb. "Lone-Elk trusted a two-faced black dog of a Paleface! That is the Seneca's crime! When the Harvest Festival was held this dog was hiding in the brushes. Big Buffalo stumbled upon him there and kicked him, like the dog that he is. They seized each other by the throats. The grip of the dog was stronger than the warrior's grip. Big Buffalo was killed. Lone-Elk has long known this. But why should he tell the Delawares? Why tell the Delawares, to save two Paleface spies, cheating and lying to the Indians and hunting on their land?

"Still, the Delawares are but squaws. They have no place among the mighty nations. Lone-Elk is glad to leave them. The Delawares will never see him again. Let them, then, tell their children that once a mighty warrior lived among them."

Not deigning to glance again toward Captain Pipe or any of the others present, but with his eyes fixed on Lobb alone, the Seneca quickly turned toward the door.

Before his intention was suspected, he swiftly raised the tomahawk in his right hand, high above his head and brought it down on the skull of the white murderer.

With a stifled cry that ended in a sickening groan, Lobb sunk to the ground, and the Indian strode haughtily into the open air, still clutching the blood-stained hatchet.

CHAPTER XXV — FAREWELL FOREVE

The killing of Lobb was as nothing to the Delawares in comparison to the words Lone-Elk had spoken, and the greatest confusion followed his sudden departure. Many Indians and two of the woodsmen rushed out as if to seize the Seneca, but he was gone. For an instant they caught sight of him among the trees, walking rapidly away, with head erect and shoulders squared. Not once did he look back.

Why no one went in pursuit of Lone-Elk might be hard to explain; but certain it is that neither Indian nor white man so much as called after him. Perhaps what was every one's business was no one's business. At any rate the Seneca went his way unmolested, and those who had hurried out after him soon returned to the Council House where, between them, Captain Pipe and Kingdom had succeeded in restoring quiet—the former by ordering the Delawares to be silent; the latter by cautioning his friends to beep cool.

Sergeant Quayle had sought to lift the unfortunate Lobb up the moment he fell, but found his task useless. The murderer was dead, and no wonder, for the gaping wound in his head was both wide and deep.

Quayle still knelt over the lifeless body when the confusion had subsided; but seeing with what horror even the savages regarded the dead man's fallen jaw and staring eyes, truly a most terrible sight, he covered the corpse with his coat.

An embarrassing silence followed the noise and commotion the tragedy had occasioned, and for a few seconds the quiet was dreadful. The Indians were in no good humor. The woodsmen were ripe and ready for trouble and Kingdom understood only too well the gravity of the situation. But he grappled with it boldly and successfully.

"Captain Pipe," he said, with quiet dignity, "A murder has been committed. A white man has been killed while under the flag of truce. It is not enough to say that he deserved his death. Of course we realize that the

176

Delawares are not exactly to blame. Still we have all learned how Big Buffalo died and we have seen the murderer punished. Now will the Delawares not agree that they no longer have a reason for holding Little Paleface a prisoner?"

"Like the Delawares have the young Paleface brothers suffered for the sins of another," Captain Pipe made answer. "They will yield the prisoner to his friends. Yet do the Delawares urge the Paleface young men to leave the lands of the Indians and, until there is peace, come back no more. They know, as the Delawares know, that it is not safe. The blood of our warriors is heated. The braves are in warpaint. For the Little Paleface and for White Fox the Delawares will have only kind thoughts. They have been good friends. The Indians have been glad to visit them and trade with them.

"Yet is it wise that they travel their separate paths alone. The ways of the Paleface are not the ways of the Indian. The Great Spirit has made them both as they are and they cannot be otherwise. Time and the conflicts that every day take place will at last draw a line between them and there will be peace and happiness. To the west will live the Indians as the Great Spirit has taught them to do. To the east, the Palefaces will cut down trees, drive off the game and build and dwell in noisy towns. It is as they have been taught. Still, only by war can the line of separation be drawn, and it is well for the Delawares and their Paleface brothers to go in different ways. Today the trail they have followed together divides. They say farewell. They hope for friendship's sake their paths may never meet in war."

With a few words in reply Kingdom hurried to John Jerome, whom the warriors quickly loosened from his bonds. The two boys clasped hands in silence.

Fishing Bird had already sent Long-Hair and Little Wolf for John's rifle and other belongings and when the lad had shaken hands with Neohaw, Gentle Maiden and Captain Pipe, his property was handed him.

Ree also took leave of the Indians whose friendship he had once enjoyed and, two of the woodsmen bearing the body of the Englishman, all the white men left the village.

Silently, their untamed spirits for the time subdued, the Indians gathered near the Council House to watch the departure of the Palefaces. To the portage trail Ree and John were accompanied by Fishing Bird. They asked him to go with them — to remain with them permanently. He shook his head.

"Paleface brothers heard the words of Captain Pipe," he said, significantly but sorrowfully, and they said good-bye forever.

An hour later, beside the portage path, the great highway of the wilderness, the body of Lobb was buried; and the sun went down and darkness enveloped the vast forest and all within it.

CHAPTER XXVI – DOWN THE SUN-KISSED SLOPE TOGETHER

Beside their campfire, near the spot where a mossy stone marked Lobb's last resting place, the two boys and their friends discussed their future movements. All were interested in visiting the murderer's camp in the ravine, and Jim Small declared his intention of making search for the Seneca's lead mine. He believed the Indian had some good reason for telling the Delawares he knew of such a mine, and, though the others did not agree with him, he held to his theory.

In substance Small's idea was that, inasmuch as out-and-out lying was not an Indian trait, Lone-Elk must have had some basis for his story more than had been discovered. However, time proved that this theory was not well founded. Jim was right in his assertion that Indians did not make lying a practice, but in this as well as in his ambition to be a leader, whatever the cost, the Seneca was less honorable than Indians were as a rule, before trickery and firewater had corrupted them.

Despite their fatigue and the day's exciting events, the woodsmen and the two boys remained awake far into the night. They were alert and watchful, however, for the older men placed no confidence whatever in the savages, and all screened themselves from sight by lying down among the bushes near which their fire was built.

Besting thus, and speaking in low tones, John told the story of his adventure and in turn heard with great interest the story of Lobb's capture and confession. There were tears in Ree's eyes when Jerome described the burning of the cabin, and for the first time he felt in his heart a hatred deep and endless toward the Indians as a whole.

The Sergeant and his men were astonished to learn of the many lively skirmishes the two pioneer boys had had with the savages at different times, and expressed their wonder that both had not been scalped long ago.

"Ye'll desarve it, too, if ever ye come to these hostyle parts ag'in," Quayle told them. "Whist! It beats all, so it do, that mere spalpeens get through where whiskers a full foot long can't go!"

The morning came, cold and raw, with a feeling of show in the air. With some haste the little party ate a breakfast of roasted smoked meat and resumed the march toward the gully. They paused for half an hour in the clearing and Ree and John soon found Neb, sheltering himself from the wind, back of a clump of bushes. Every particle of harness had been destroyed by the fire, and only a strip of buckskin could be found wherewith to lead the horse. Neb was very docile, however, and upon his willing back a roughly fashioned pack was soon placed. It contained corn and potatoes from the fields the boys had cultivated, and various articles of baggage of which the woodsmen were glad to be relieved.

Before leaving the clearing Ree and John went again to the heap of ashes which marked the cabin site. Together they surveyed the ruins and were glad of the opportunity to speak to each other some words of sympathy their companions would not hear. As they did so, John noticed sticking in the half-burned end of a log a blood-stained tomahawk.

"Look! Lone-Elk came here!" he said.

"I declare," returned Kingdom solemnly, "his hatred is something almost more than human. Venting his feelings by leaving that hatchet at this spot! I suppose he intends it as a warning!"

Neither boy was disposed to touch the weapon and they left it—left it and the remnants of their fallen hopes and castles among the ashes of the cabin. Ree sighed as they turned away. "But still," he said, brightening, "we have enough to be thankful for, after all."

It was nearly noon when the camp in the gully was reached. Apparently no one had been near since the capture of Lobb, and no reason to doubt the truthfulness of the story the guilty wretch had told could be discovered, excepting that no gold was found.

"We'd orter got that 'fore we took the heathen away," said one of the woodsmen, and the others agreed.

Ree and John, however, did not greatly care. With the others, they made careful search of the vicinity, however. Nothing did they find except a few articles of food, some cooking utensils, a bullet mold and a quantity of lead and powder in the low, shallow cave concealed among the bushes. All the afternoon was given up to hunting for the lead mine and the gold thought to be hidden near by. But the Seneca's mine, if he had one, remains undiscovered to this day. Neither was the slightest trace of the treasure sent for the Indians, but who never received it, found.

The searchers made camp at night near the hollow whitewood, whose sheltering trunk protected Ree, John and the Sergeant. The others scoffed good-naturedly, saying the first three were no better than bears. Nevertheless the tree was a very comfortable place, and especially on this occasion, for during the night much snow fell.

The desirability of reaching Wayne's camp as soon as possible was apparent to all members of the party and rapid marching was agreed upon. A halt of a half day for hunting, with the result that a quantity of fresh venison and several turkeys were carried into camp, was the only delay in the journey to the east, and the distance of nearly one hundred miles was covered in a little more than five days.

Gen. Wayne sent for both Kingdom and Jerome the day following their arrival and from them heard a full account of the salt springs murder, the death of Lobb, and the indisputable evidence that the British at Detroit were extending aid to the redskins throughout the Northwest territory. He cautioned the boys that they must not think of returning to their clearing, and, thinking perhaps of the military ambitions of his own boyhood, the sham battles he had arranged and fought, and the sieges he had planned, asked them if they would like to join his "Legion." It was by this name that he always called the army he was assembling.

Thanking him, and saying they would like to think of his offer and talk it over, the lads took leave of the great soldier, feeling very well satisfied with themselves.

In the end, however, Ree and John did not join the "Legion." They were not lacking in courage, nor in patriotism. But within the next few days John was taken very sick. The injuries and exposure he had suffered were the cause of it, the army surgeon said. He was removed to Fort Pitt and the winter was half over before he was again able to be out of doors. He regained strength slowly and with the coming of spring he and Ree, mounted on Neb and Phoebe, made the trip by easy stages to Connecticut. Three years passed before the boys went west again, and along the whole frontier peace reigned supreme. Wayne's victory over the savages at the Battle of Fallen Timbers effectually ended their resistance to civilization's advance in the Ohio country, and never again did a serious outbreak occur in the region named. By the treaty of Fort Greenville in 1796 the extreme eastern boundary between the settlers and the Indians was definitely fixed at the Cuyahoga and Tuscarawas rivers and the portage path. It so remained until the treaty of Fort Industry in 1805 when the Indians sold the lands west of the path and the rivers named.

The village of Captain Pipe on the little lake had by this time long since disappeared. As a nation the Delawares were scattered and their numbers were small. Eventually they found homes in a far western reservation.

Although Ree and John never saw the honest, loyal Fishing Bird again, they heard of him as taking a gallant part, on the side of the Indians, of course, in the Battle of Fallen Timbers. Report reached them also of a most bitterly hostile savage who was among the killed in this battle. He fought with his last breath. Though shot twice through the body, he raised himself on his elbow and sunk his knife into a wounded soldier who had fallen near him. That this redskin was Lone-Elk, the Seneca, there can be little doubt.

There is a tradition that the beautiful daughter of Captain Pipe so attracted a young warrior, whose admiration she did not like, that he poisoned himself when she rejected his attentions. Another tradition states that Gentle Maiden was cruelly shot by two white men, while walking alone in the woods. I do not know whether these legends are supported by fact nor do I know if there is any truth whatever in the tradition of there having been a lead mine in the Cuyahoga valley, the existence of which was known only to the Indians.

Return Kingdom and John Jerome did not settle again where their original clearing had been.

There was a reason and it was that pretty Mary Catesby, a very early friend of Ree's, having become Mrs. Return Kingdom, was a party to the plans for the permanent removal west. She wanted to be somewhere within reach of neighbors.

Woman-like, she had her way, and Ree bought land near Marietta. Where Kingdom was John Jerome was sure to be, and he owned the adjoining farm.

Both the boys, now to manhood grown, were active in the public affairs of the state of Ohio, organized a few years later, and many a day and evening found them together in conference concerning matters of mutual interest.

They did not always agree, but it is certain they never quarreled. Their lives were blessed with many quiet joys and even when sorrows came they also were shared and each grief and burden seemed the lighter.

More and more often in later years, as the two went down the sun-kissed slope of lives well spent did they speak of the adventures of their youth. Maybe John was inclined to brag a little.

Some say so. But both were liked by all.

To the end of his days John looked up to Ree as to an elder brother, and if he did brag it was of Kingdom's exploits, rather than his own, and the latter was wont to smile, "Well, well! They were days quite brisk enough, and pleasant now to talk about; but in quite a different way the present days are brisker, after all."

THE END.

Milton Keynes UK
Ingram Content Group UK Ltd.
UKHW040902181023
430840UK00004B/175